"I can't let you on my aircraft," Mark said.

"Stop trying to control me. I won't be meek Cassie again."

He wanted her to be bold, too. How could he argue against that?

Bending his head, he found the beat of her pulse and he brushed his lips against it. "What if we forget everything else for tonight and just..."

Her lips curled into a sexy, sassy smile, then she shouted a challenge and took off. Her long hair flew behind her as she raced down to the water, and excitement surged and he sprinted after her.

Just before she reached the water, he grabbed her waist and swung her around. Their laughter rang out, then faded when he turned her in his arms and lowered her slowly along the length of his body, feeling every luscious inch of her.

He placed his hands around her face and pulled it gently to him. "You're not meek," he whispered against her mouth.

"What am I, then?"

"Mine," he groaned, and his mouth captured hers. He didn't know if he could protect her from the storm tomorrow, but he could shelter her tonight, comfort her the only way he knew how...

Dear Reader,

Everyone has dealt with loss. Sometimes we face it head-on. Other times, it's so far down, we deny ourselves the chance to ever fully heal. But generally when we're forced to deal with our regrets—and we always are—the path to understanding, acceptance and forgiveness isn't as unpassable as we expect. When someone truly loves us, they open our hearts and help us to let go of a dark past to embrace a brighter future. Suddenly we see that we have so much to live for, starting with the person who wouldn't give up on us, who believed, even when we didn't, that we were worthy of happiness and love. Together.

As you can imagine, that road isn't an easy one to travel for LCDR Mark Sampson and Cassie Rowe, RN. The grieving nurse and the tortured USCG pilot she blames for her brother's loss can't resist their combustible passion during their hurricane mission. But will they find the closure and healing they need in each other's arms and make it through the storm at last?

I hope you enjoy *His to Protect*. Be sure to look for my next Uniformly Hot! novel, book two in my USCG No Defenses series, *At His Command*, in spring 2017. I'd love to hear from you at karenrock.com. or come chat with me on Twitter, @KarenRock5 or Facebook, at Facebook.com/karenrockwrites.

Best wishes,

Karen

Karen Rock is an award-winning young adult and adult contemporary author. She holds a master's degree in English and worked as an ELA instructor before becoming a full-time author. Most recently, her Harlequin Heartwarming novels have won the 2015 National Excellence in Romance Fiction Award and the 2015 Booksellers' Best Award. When she's not writing, Karen loves scouring estate sales, cooking and hiking. She lives in the Adirondack Mountain region with her husband, daughter and Cavalier King Charles spaniels. Visit her at karenrock.com.

Books by Karen Rock

Harlequin Heartwarming

Wish Me Tomorrow
His Hometown Girl
Someone Like You
A League of Her Own
Raising the Stakes
Winter Wedding Bells
"The Kiss"
His Kind of Cowgirl
Under an Adirondack Sky

To get the inside scoop on Harlequin Blaze and its talented writers, visit Facebook.com/BlazeAuthors.

All backlist available in ebook format.

Visit the author profile page at Harlequin.com for more titles.

This book is dedicated to the top emergency-response unit in the world, the USCG Air and Sea Rescue personnel. They routinely put the lives of others before their own, applying intense physical and mental training to challenging real-world situations where there's often no margin for error. These brave men and women embody the courage of America's Coast Guard, readily going into harm's way to complete their rescue missions in some of the most extreme environments imaginable.

Our world is a safer place because of their selflessness, dedication and bravery. They personify the Coast Guard's motto, *Semper Paratus*, "Always Prepared." I'm deeply grateful for their sacrifice and inspired by their service. Special thanks to CDR Bill Friday, USCG Jayhawk pilot and trainer, who gave me incredible insight and provided intimate details into the rigors of this challenging profession.

1

Had she lost her damn mind?

Cassie Rowe ignored the question looping in her head and checked the time on her cell phone. Nearly midnight. Her throat swelled. Only six hours until she boarded a US Coast Guard helicopter as a first-time Red Cross volunteer to help the hurricane-ravaged Virgin Islands and honor her lost brother. Unless she chickened out...

Her jittering knee smacked the bottom of the wooden table inside Mayday's Bar & Grill and she clamped a hand on it. She'd come all this way and wasn't about to turn tail now.

She peered around the crowded, nautical-themed bar, the hard-thumping rock music no match for the service personnel and other volunteers ready to ship out of Clearwater with her in a large-scale relief effort. They laughed and flirted in shadowed corners, their grinding silhouettes on the dance floor causing Cassie to experience an unexpected spike of arousal. Her life in small-town Idaho discouraged casual hookups even if she'd had the time. How long since she'd had sex?

Too long.

She toyed with the miniature anchor on her charm bracelet, figuring her love life would have to remain dormant awhile longer. Tonight wasn't about hooking up. She'd only come here to pass a couple of hours since she probably wouldn't be able to sleep. She'd need some serious courage tomorrow morning to hitch a ride on the same type of aircraft that'd carried her rescue-swimmer brother on a similar mission a year ago…then left him to die alone at sea.

Anger pulsed through her harder than the thumping bass. How could it have happened? Going on this mission, she hoped, would finally give her some answers. And, maybe, honor her brother's life and wishes. He'd challenged her to break out of her safe world back home. Live a little. And she'd hesitated. Jeff had been the daring older sibling she'd admired but never thought she could emulate. While he'd never given risk a thought, she mulled over possibilities until she wound up doing nothing at all.

Until now.

She raised his favorite drink—rum and cola—and toasted him. How she missed Jeff. That solid, big-brother presence she'd always thought she could count on.

Damn it. Grief still snuck up on her at odd times, surprising her with its force. Shoving to her feet, she smoothed down her dress and eased out of the booth. Might as well head back to her quarters since the bar hadn't distracted her from her thoughts after all. Leaving a fat tip for the waitress, Cassie turned to go and bumped into a hard masculine shoulder.

"Excuse me," she muttered, swiveling her hips sideways to pass the wall of lean muscle.

"Sorry" came the terse response.

Topaz eyes locked with hers for an instant, the barest connection with a stranger. And then, he was gone. She hovered there for a moment, oddly affected by that disarming gaze from beneath a dark tangle of hair, buzzed at the sides. The handsome mouth that'd curved above a square jaw. A slow shiver tripped along her skin, so foreign that it took her a long moment to recognize the sensation for what it was. Attraction.

Raw and simple. Totally unexpected.

Giving herself a shake, she headed toward the door again, only to remember the feel of the man's eyes on her once more.

She'd come to the bar for a distraction, hadn't she? And, much to her surprise, she'd just found one. Maybe she needed to start honoring that promise to her brother now. Tonight. After all, she hadn't come all this way just to find answers about his death.

She was also here to take risks. Stop second-guessing herself. Live a little. And the gorgeous stranger might be her chance to do just that.

USCG Jayhawk helicopter pilot Lieutenant Commander Mark Sampson shoved through the crowd, brain still stuck on the deer-in-the-headlights look he'd just seen on the mouthwatering blonde. Those wide, serious blue eyes seemed out of sync with this hard-drinking, hard-partying military crowd.

Not that he had any business chasing beautiful women tonight or even being out. Not when he had wheels up in six hours for a mission that called to him, a mission he needed like he needed air. He'd spent too much time on the ground lately, definitely punishment for a guy who craved action. Adrenaline. The job.

Didn't matter that there was a major storm system threatening to rain all kinds of hell on his head. He'd been waiting for two days for the worst of the hurricane to pass before they were approved to fly into the Virgin Islands. Time crawled when he wasn't in the air, his mind on his job and nothing else. He needed to clock more hours in the cockpit and stay in the bubble—stay focused—to put some time between him and his past, and not even a gorgeous blonde would be able to fix that.

He sat at a corner table alone. When he brought the flat of his hand down on the table, empty beer bottles jumped. He dropped his head into his palms and felt the throb at his temples. Coming here had been a mistake. The happy crowd couldn't dispel his demons.

He should be at the hotel room the overcrowded base had booked him into when his Elizabeth City, North Carolina, crew had arrived to provide rescue support during the hurricane. He'd head back and organize his emergency response gear soon.

Once he finished his soda, he'd leave.

A moment later, a slap thudded against his back. Ian, a crew member and close friend since his academy days, twirled and straddled a chair.

"Sticking to the hard stuff I see." Ian grinned as he pointed to the soda can near Mark's glass.

"No juice for the pilot. How about you? Want a drink?" Mark raised his voice as a Jimmy Buffett tune switched over to hard rock.

"Nah. I'm heading out. Dylan's my ride and he's got

his panties in a bunch. Just found out he's transferring to Kodiak when he gets back from Saint Thomas."

Mark searched his memory, something nagging at him about Dylan, another rescue swimmer he'd flown when they'd been training. Then it hit him. "Isn't Dylan from Alaska?"

Ian nodded. "Some bad blood there, though. A woman. At least that's what he was mumbling about before the bartender cut him off. Looks like I'm the DD." Mark followed Ian's glance to Dylan, who paced by the bar's exit. "Besides, better get some shut-eye before the big show."

"They're calling it the storm of the century." Mark swirled the ice cubes in his glass, making them clank together.

Ian leaned his elbows on the table and lowered his voice. "Doing okay?"

Mark jerked his chin up and down while his stomach clenched. "I've got it."

His demons were off-limits.

Ian thumped him on the back again and stood. "Thought so." He stretched his long arms overhead and a couple of lurking women nudged each other and pointed. "See you on the beach."

A mirthless laugh escaped Mark. "Yep. Don't forget the sunscreen."

With a wave Ian ambled away, trailed by a couple of women. Mark shook his head and lifted his drink.

"Mind if I join you?" asked a silky voice from behind him.

He peered up into the crystal-blue eyes that'd nearly snared him earlier. God. She was an eyeful in an off-the-shoulder short white dress that made him want to slip the elastic neckline lower…or that hemline higher…

Long blond hair shone like a beacon in the dark bar. The woman was classically beautiful but carried herself like she had no clue. She fidgeted with a bracelet and bit her lip as if she was unsure of her reception. Like there was any chance in hell a guy might say no to her.

He swiped away the discarded beer bottles the waitress hadn't gotten around to picking up from the previous occupants.

"Seat's all yours." His gaze wandered over her tanned legs before she dropped into the spot beside him.

She wound her thick hair into a messy topknot, and repositioned a patterned headband to hold things in place. "Wow, this place is packed," she said, waving her hand in front of her flushed face. "We must be breaking some fire codes."

As she glanced around the room, his eyes lingered on the profile revealed by her upswept do. Everything about her face was soft and round, from her large blue eyes, to the delicate tip of her nose, and the tender-looking flesh beneath her slightly jutting chin. His fingers itched to touch it.

"Mayday's has seen worse than this. Is it your first time here?"

"What gave me away?" She did a little eye roll, a self-deprecating gesture that charmed him more than a practiced come-on.

"Most of the regulars don't bother with conversation." He pointed out a couple on the dance floor whose groping session was leaving them both overexposed.

"Oh." She blinked and he'd bet money she blushed,

but it was too dark to tell for sure. "How nice for them." She toasted them with her mostly empty drink.

"I'm Mark." He held out a hand, unable to resist the excuse to touch her.

"Cassie." She set down her glass and wiped her hand on a cocktail napkin before folding her fingers around his.

Her touch was cool and impossibly soft, her charm bracelet grazing his skin before she pulled away. The tug of arousal he felt was immediate and too strong to ignore. Which meant sitting with her tonight was going to be more than a distraction.

"Cassie, I'll be honest with you." He didn't want to mislead her and he didn't know if he could rein himself in when she stirred this kind of response. "I'm not the best company tonight—"

"Maybe you should let me be the judge of that." Her blue eyes met his head-on with a look that wasn't quite as innocent, the self-consciousness he'd detected earlier giving way to a mix of teasing determination.

In fact, he suspected this awkward beauty was flirting with him.

He felt his lips twitch. "You think?"

"I'm definitely no bar scene expert, but I know what intrigues a woman. I can be a fair judge."

"And how exactly are you making your evaluation?"

He might be on edge tonight, but that wasn't her problem. Besides, something about this woman shrunk the shadows inside him. He'd linger a little longer. Find out more about her.

She leaned in close and he inhaled her honey-and-vanilla scent. This near, he could make out the pale freckles sprinkled across her nose.

"Well." She tapped her chin thoughtfully. "Let's get the superficial out of the way first and judge you on your looks."

The soda burned as he swallowed the wrong way. He appreciated a direct woman. Didn't encounter as many as he'd like, though. "And how am I doing?"

"On a ten-point scale?" Her eyes slid along the length of him and lingered on his mouth long enough to raise his temperature, his libido firing. "I'd say a nine."

"And what did I lose a point on?" He shouldn't be here, flirting with a woman who didn't have nearly enough hard edges to be a part of his world. But she amused him. And if he left, who would be looking out for her?

She shrugged sun-kissed shoulders, making the left sleeve slide nearly to her elbow. His mouth flooded. A hungry dog drooling over a juicy bone. "Not much, really. But I couldn't inflate your ego more by giving you a perfect score on your looks."

"Who said I have an ego?"

She laughed, a tinkling, bubbling sound that sparked like a flare inside him. "Puh-lease. A woman sees confidence on a man from a mile away."

A smile maneuvered its way around his face. A damned unfamiliar feeling. "Point taken. Next category?"

"Then we'd move on to more important things. Like humor."

"Can I throw out the judge's highest and lowest scores?"

"I'm your judge and your jury." She pointed a swizzle stick at him. "But since that was sort of funny, I'll let you slide with a seven point five."

"I'll take it." With his mood, he would have scored himself a lot lower, although the night didn't seem half as dark with Cassie across the table from him. "Is your next category about money?"

"You think that's all women care about?" She glanced over her shoulder as she said the words, her gaze taking in the men waving green bills at the bartender. "The size of your wallet?"

"That and the size of our—"

"Regardless," she interrupted. "I was thinking the next category would be *class*."

Another sip of soda polished off his drink. He should leave, but with the alluring, teasing woman beside him, he was no longer sure he wanted to escape. "What's my number?"

"An eight. You lose two for not offering me a cocktail as soon as I sat down." Her impish grin reappeared and his body tightened at the small, sexy space between her front teeth. "You must have known I was nervous."

He wondered why a beautiful woman would be nervous about sharing his table, but she seemed relaxed enough now. He didn't want that smile of hers to fade.

"I hope it's not too late to fix that." He waved over the waitress hovering on the edge of the crowd. "A drink for the lady."

Cassie frowned. "I wasn't going to drink any more tonight. But maybe just one." Glancing up at the server, she quizzed her on the tequila choices before deciding. "Margarita on the rocks, salt not sugar."

"Not sweet, then?" he teased once they were alone again, enjoying this time with the woman keeping him on his toes and out of his dark thoughts.

"Sweetness doesn't get you far in life, I've learned."

Shadows crossed through her blue gaze for a moment, but then she blinked and the look disappeared. "I'm cultivating a tart side."

"You'll need that if you decide to spend much time at Mayday's." He didn't like thinking about her here without him, though. He changed topics fast. "Next category?"

"Power." Her lips pursed as she considered him, the move making him uncomfortably aware of the fullness of her mouth. "You're a ten."

His pulse slugged hard, this flirtation ratcheting up the heat in a hurry.

"A perfect score."

She biffed his bicep. "Really? Like you don't notice the waitresses falling over themselves to obey your every command?"

As if to underscore her words, the server hustled back with the beverage.

"Would you?" he asked once they were alone again, the words leaving his mouth before he could stop them.

She sucked slowly on a lime wedge, each second of silence building the tension between them. "That remains to be seen," she said at last.

Which was definitely not a no. Damn but she was keeping him guessing.

"Depending on…?" He balled his hands on his thighs then forced his fingers to relax. Why push this? He had every intention of leaving. With his drink finished, he was out of excuses to dawdle with this tempting woman. He blamed his mouth. Always open one sentence too long.

"How you score in the rest of my categories," she countered, leaning closer. The move outlined full breasts beneath the gauzy fabric of her dress as her long, silky legs appeared and disappeared when she uncrossed them.

He looked away, beating back the sexual attraction firing through him. He hadn't expected this tonight. Definitely not from a woman like Cassie.

"And how many more are there?" A throaty growl had entered his voice, an impatient sound, a hunger he couldn't hide behind some teasing word game.

"Just one."

He kept his eyes on the bouncers setting up a row of chairs on the emptying dance floor. Forced his focus off her tongue as she swiped at the salt on the rim of her glass.

"You've got me on the edge of my seat here," he admitted, thinking more time with Cassie could make the hours between now and the next mission disappear.

Better yet, she might make those hours better than just bearable. He hadn't allowed himself that kind of pleasure since…

A stab of pain behind his eyes reminded him exactly how long it had been. To the day. The hour.

She reached out a hand and covered his wrist.

"You okay?" The flirtatious look had vanished, making him realize he'd be an ass to walk away from this chance to exorcise a few demons tonight.

"I could be better," he started, ready to detail exactly how.

But just then the damn DJ stepped forward and the crowd hushed. "Ladies, it's time to grab a partner for our lap dance contest. The longer you keep from touching your male dancer, the longer the couple stays in.

The woman with the most—er—control, takes home this magnum of champagne…and your man."

The guy hefted a bottle larger than his head.

Cassie lifted her eyebrows in question. Almost as if to ask him if that kind of game was a possibility. Something about her expression made his lower abs contract with swift, fierce need. Was she teasing him? He had a sudden urge to discover where she drew the line with this flirtation.

While the crowd responded to the DJ's provocation, he flipped his hand so he was holding Cassie's.

"So what's that last category?" he pressed.

He squinted at her until her cheeks pinked and she squirmed. He wanted to haul her out of the bar and back to his room, where he could lose himself in that incredible body and mind-numbing sex.

But even if he was the type for casual hookups, something about her didn't speak of one-night stands… despite her flirting. Maybe it was the pain tucked in the corners of her laughing eyes, the way her smiles slid off her face too fast, as if they rarely stuck. He was having a tough time reading her.

"It's one I'm not prepared to judge just yet." Her words were breathless.

He could feel the thrum of her pulse where he held her hand, the pace a rapid tattoo of nerves or excitement. Or something more.

"Now I'm even more curious." He slid a thumb along the heart of her palm and imagined himself touching other parts of her that same way. With slow, lazy circles. "You can at least tell me what you would be critiquing."

Her blues met and held his. No innocence there now. Only heat and daring.

"Sexual prowess." She drew out the words like a long caress.

His whole body hardened like new-forged steel and just as hot.

They stared at each other across the table, the noisy world of the bar full of lap dancers not even a blip on his radar. He breathed in when Cassie exhaled, their shared air as hot as any kiss he'd ever tasted.

"You ready to cut out of here?" he asked, his voice low and his restraint disappearing.

He wanted nothing more than to drive her wild and fill her head with enough sexy dreams to satisfy her for the rest of the night. He tossed bills on the table, never taking his eyes off her.

She squeezed his hand. "I thought you'd never ask."

2

LIVE A LITTLE?

Cassie cursed herself as she followed the tall, gorgeous stranger through the bar and out a side door that led onto the beach. Surely this was going too far, playing teasing games with a man she hardly knew after inviting herself to share his table. "Live a little" didn't mean she should allow some alien consciousness to inhabit her body and make her say crazy, sexually charged things. Where the hell was her sense? Her reliable Midwestern restraint? The second-guessing?

But as she gripped Mark's hand and allowed the warmth of his touch to seep into her skin, she couldn't deny that he inspired something hot and raw inside her. An edgy, hungry feeling she'd never experienced before. What was it about him that made her take risks? Flirt wildly? Follow him out onto the beach…alone.

The funny part was, she trusted him more than she trusted herself. He hadn't consumed any alcohol, for one thing, so she was certain he had his head screwed on straight. For another, she knew he had to be a military guy and that inspired a certain level of confidence. Especially here, in a town full of his peers. Plus, he hadn't dragged her out onto the dance floor for the obvious bump and grind that some couples engaged in. All they'd done was talk, even when she'd been thinking wickedly explicit things about him back in that bar...

"It's beautiful here," Mark observed suddenly, face turned up to stargaze. They passed sweat-slicked men engrossed in a volleyball game under a flickering fluorescent lamp.

"And so warm." She shivered as she said it, savoring the kiss of the Gulf breeze on her skin.

"You want to go for a walk?" He dropped his gaze back to her and she appreciated that he hadn't simply shuttled her off to a hotel room after their suggestive game.

She needed to catch her breath.

"I'd like that." Her heart beat a strange tempo when he slid his fingers from her chin and along her cheek, tracing the sensitive skin there, his gaze never leaving hers.

There was a brief silence, interrupted by the cry of gulls hovering over them. Mark looked at her for a few drawn-out seconds, the heat in his eyes making her shiver. Then he reached out a hand. "Let's go this way."

His fingers twined with hers and goose bumps rose on her arms as they strolled to the water.

Ahead of them the surf pulsed, rushing and foaming on the sand. Beach roses lined their path down to the shore, the smell faint and sweet in the salty air. She looked up at the sky. So many stars, it seemed like a celebration, a fireworks display just for them.

She slid a sideways glance at him, taking in his chiseled profile. Noted the firm set of his jaw, his straight nose and strong brow. Features that exuded authority. Confidence. Security. The kind of face you'd want to see if you needed rescuing.

Her grief for Jeff fell away under the solid presence of Mark walking beside her. And she needed that tonight. Something about him made her feel different. Stronger. Sexier.

If she scurried back to her hotel room, she knew exactly what to expect. Nothing. Yet out here, with the wind gusting off the water, seabirds calling, salt water misting her face, a deep hunger stirred inside her. A wild thirst for the unknown.

Crazy or not, this was what her brother had wanted for her. To experience life on a large scale, well beyond the neat world she'd organized for herself back in Idaho.

Suddenly, warm water rushed across her feet and over her ankles. She gasped and stepped closer to shore then stopped when Mark's arm came around her. He turned her toward him. Her hands landed on his lean waist, her fingers grazing his contracting stomach muscles beneath the crisp cotton of his T-shirt.

"I didn't think the water came up this far."

"The tide's rising." His voice was thick, distracted, as heat flared in his eyes.

"Oh," she mumbled, her mouth dry, her body warm.

He reached out and stroked her hair, his gaze full of promise and something more. "Are you sure you want to keep going?"

She understood what he was asking her. Appreciated that he'd given her some time to think. To be certain about the attraction and where it was headed.

But even with the fresh air to clear her thoughts, she still wanted him. Still craved the chance to feel all that warm male strength around her before she embarked on the most dangerous adventure of her life.

"Absolutely." She slid her hand up his abdomen, teasing the hard ridges that moved and shifted beneath her touch. His chest rose sharply when her fingers rested on her pecs. Exhilaration forked through her.

"Cassie," he groaned, stepping closer so that her feet brushed his in the shifting sand.

She rose on her toes and cupped her hands around the base of his neck, pulling his mouth to hers.

Bodies fusing at the same moment as their lips, nerve endings fired faster than the incoming tide. Hip to hip, breast to chest, her body curved into his, molding around all that hard, hot muscle. Pleasure tingled along her nerve endings, making her wriggle closer and sigh into his kiss.

She felt a low groan vibrate through his chest, but she didn't hear it, the rush of waves drowning out everything else. Her breath caught at the back of her throat, her senses heightened. Every facet of the kiss imprinted itself on her consciousness, burrowing into her memory as if it would never leave.

He placed his hands on either side of her temples and kissed her gently, easing back ever so slightly. He traced her lips slowly with his tongue, then sucked on her lower lip in a way that made tension coil between her thighs. She wanted him. Wanted this.

But they were still too close to the bar.

Breaking the kiss, she whispered against his mouth, "Should we find somewhere more private?" Her dress rode up where she leaned into him, the denim on his thighs caressing her bare legs in a way that made her ache.

"Definitely." Turning, he peered into the dark and pointed toward a sandy mound covered in sea oats with a shadowed area at the base.

There were no buildings. No lights.

"Let's check it out." She was already pulling him across the beach, calculating how fast she could have him all to herself. And then another thought occurred to her.

"Wait." She stopped, kicking up sand as she spun. Her hand caught him midchest, halting him, too.

"I'm going to honor your wishes, no matter." He sucked in a deep breath. "But I gotta say, I'd hoped we passed the 'wait' stage a while ago."

"Me, too." She licked her lips. "But I don't have anything—that is, protectionwise—with me."

"No worries." His teeth flashed white in the darkness. "I've got that covered."

Giddy relief lit her up inside and her smile matched his. A laugh bubbled up and she dragged him toward the sandy dunes. They reached the privacy of the sheltered area, where he stifled her laughter with hungry kisses, his hands entwined in her hair, his mouth warm on her lips. She kissed him back hard, not hesitating even when they heard voices from a boat out on the water, the dunes and sea oats hiding them from view. The space provided a private, intimate hideaway.

Closing her eyes, she tunneled her hands under his shirt, giving in to the insistent rush of pleasure that had started with the first accidental brush of their bodies. Now she could touch him. Taste him.

Their kisses grew deeper, more urgent. She wanted

to feel his bare skin against hers, so she dragged his shirt up and off his broad shoulders. She opened her eyes to see what she'd unveiled.

So. Fine.

Her hands moved to his waist, resting on the band of his jeans, ready for more. But then he stepped into her, his kiss hotter. Harder. She could feel how much he wanted her and she shifted her hips to cradle that hard length against her softness. Things were escalating fast and that's just what she wanted. More. Faster.

Mark.

THE FEEL OF Cassie's hips pressed to his wiped his brain of any last remnant of thought. There was only him, her and the heat of this longing.

If he didn't take her soon, he would explode. He broke off, his hands on her face, and saw her eyes, heavy with longing. Her lips parted, her chest rising and falling rapidly. He cupped the back of her head, wrapping an arm around her shoulders before easing her down onto the warm sand.

"Mark," she gasped, reaching for him. But he knew having her hands on him would only drive him faster. And she deserved better than a tumble in the dark.

He lay on his side instead and undid the button at the top of her dress. He worked his way down that trail of fastenings, forcing himself to take his time. His fingers fumbled, unsteady, when he reached the final enclosure at her hem and parted the material. He drew it off her shoulders and down her arms, tugging her hands free so that she lay on top of the dress, naked except for a lace bra and panties.

His muscles twisted. Pulsed.

She was incredible.

The lush curves of her breasts rose and fell beneath her bra, her nipples straining against the fabric. Electricity sparked through his veins as he traced one nipple, then the other, a sigh whispering in the air as she arched into his hand. His mouth went dry then flooded with moisture. Desire ran rampant through his body, filming it in a light sheen.

He flicked open the front clasp of her bra and the sight of her full, round breasts knocked the air from his lungs. Made his chest burn. Need and craving pounded through him. He groaned as he palmed their satisfying weight and filled his large hands with their petal-soft flesh. When he lowered his mouth and circled her nipples with his tongue, tugging lightly on the hard buds, Cassie whimpered. She tasted of spun sugar, and her honey-and-vanilla scent, combined with the fresh sea air, scrambled his thoughts.

There was no denying she was as turned on as he was. He could read it in the hungry glow of her eyes, the flush of her skin and the way she squirmed beneath his touch. She undulated her hips, ribs and spine as if urging him to explore. And he didn't need the encouragement. The grip on his control slipped further still, her effect on him devastating and bone deep. He kissed her with greater urgency, murmuring her name.

He traced her slender rib cage hungrily, the inward turn of her waist and the delicate flare of her hips before drawing an invisible line down her quivering abdomen. At the lacy top of her panties he paused, then slid his hand slowly beneath the material.

Her head tipped back and her eyes closed as she groaned again, her response jolting him with pleasure. His hand cupped her sex, lingering over its wet warmth. Dampness flooded his fingers as he stroked her hot, silken flesh. The metal teeth of his zipper bit into his straining erection. Blood rushed to his groin and made him light-headed.

Her moans deepened, and she gasped when he circled her clit with his thumb. He thrust a finger inside her and stroked gently in and out. Her tight flesh clamped around him, making him imagine how it'd feel around his cock... Yet he held himself in check. Wanted to pleasure her first. Chase away the last of those shadows that'd lingered in her eyes.

He delved deeper and she shuddered, back arching and hips thrusting forward, her chest rising and falling fast. She cried out and convulsed as she pressed against his hand. Hard. Then she collapsed, limp in the sand. With her face damp and flushed, her glittering eyes unfocused, she looked every bit as sated as he wanted her to be. As he wanted to be. He blinked down at her, the pressure of his desire licking through his blood.

Her burning cheek rested against Mark's rigid shoulder and her ragged breathing gradually slowed. Not wanting to rush her, he held himself in check—barely. Kept his balled hands at his sides. Waited. And waited. When he felt her fingers slowly lower his bulging zipper, he shuddered.

Her cool fingers wrapped around his aching erection, gently skimming the length. It took every ounce of focus not to explode in her hands like a teenager. Jesus. She drove him crazy. His guttural moan seemed to encourage her mind-blowing quest. Her fingers circled his damp tip, teasing, before trailing down his rigid shaft to cup the swelling sack below.

Time to end this torture. He yanked off his jeans
and shirt, removed the condom he kept in his wallet, ripped open the foil package and rolled the sheath
down his cock.

"You feel so good," he groaned as he slid over her.
Her legs lifted around his waist as he nudged her satin
opening with his tip.

"Yes," she breathed as he thrust home, filling her
up, drowning her in sensation.

They came together slowly then faster and faster,
her hold on him tightening, his lips grazing her skin,
her breath ragged in his ear. As her movements grew
more violent, he returned them, pulling out then burying himself in her again and again. His hips thrust pow-
erfully and she tightened around him with every stroke.

Incredible. Mind-blowing. Sensational.

He leaned back on his heels and leveraged her up
onto his lap, their bodies remaining joined. Her thighs
straddled him as she rocked back and forth against his
near-bursting hardness. He cupped her ass and kneaded
its firm flesh, pressing her even closer, his cock buried to the hilt.

When she rose up and plunged down, he slipped to
the edge, about to lose control. He wanted to prolong
this moment. Savor it. Draw out each mouth-watering
sensation, but it was beyond him. Instead, he held her
tight, lifting and lowering her, over and over, faster
and faster, their hips meeting frantically.

Their synchronized motion increased to a frenzied,
heart-stopping tempo. Her breath came in fast, urgent
pants that intensified until he heard the cry build at
the back of her throat. When her head tipped back,
he stopped her shriek with his mouth, absorbing the

sound, her pleasure, so surely that it became his own. Her bouncing breasts, tight spasms and the surf pounding the beach in unison with his thrusts were suddenly too much. He exploded within her, the darkness inside him evaporating at this incredible release.

They fell back to the ground, limbs tangling, chests heaving, his arm around her shoulders as he pressed her close. She shivered, limp in his arms as they held each other.

When their breathing returned to normal, she raised herself on her elbow and looked down at him. Something in her had altered: her features had lifted, the strain had vanished from around her eyes.

An unnamed emotion rolled through him, more satisfying, even, than this mind-blowing physical release. He'd eased her troubles as surely as she'd made him forget his own. He enclosed her in his arms again, pulling her to him so tightly that their bodies molded to one another, her soft curves fitting into his rough edges.

Just hours ago, she'd been a stranger but now... now...well, he couldn't put a label on it. Just knew that he'd seek her out after the mission. See where this amazing thing between them might lead.

His train of thought was broken by her kissing his chest, his shoulder, his neck, with intense concentration. "You realize," he said, rolling her over so that her legs were entwined with his, her mouth inches away, "that we're going to have to do that again."

"God. I hope so," she sighed, her lids closing, a dimple appearing as her mouth curled up.

"Want to go for a swim first? I'll wash you off."

A wicked light appeared when her eyes snapped

open, the color silver in the moonlight. "I'll give you extra points if you can get the sand out of my hair."

At the vision of his hands all over her naked body in the water, he hardened again. Before he let himself get too distracted, he got to his feet and held out a hand.

"I'm still waiting for my scores on sexual prowess," he murmured, gathering her close.

"Are you kidding me?" She skimmed a hand along his hip and pressed her lips to his bare chest. "That number was off the charts."

Just like that, he was ready for her all over again. He didn't know how he was going to walk away from her before the sun rose, but he'd sure as hell make the most of every minute before then.

3

CASSIE SNAPPED AN elastic band around her damp hair the next morning as she rode the transport bus to the Coast Guard base. Outside, the dark sky had barely lightened to charcoal and humid air moved sluggishly through the vents. Not the most promising of sunrises. The day looked stormy already.

Yesterday, she might have worried about the bad omen of those clouds overhead. Now, with her limbs pleasantly sore from an overdose of pleasure last night, she felt too languid and satisfied to panic. Amazing what a night of mind-blowing sex would do for a woman. After their swim, they'd headed back to Mark's hotel, where they'd made love until an hour ago. They'd parted ways in the parking lot, kissing right up until the moment when she'd turned her key in her ignition.

There hadn't been any promises to call. And not until she'd reached her room did she realize she hadn't even gotten his last name. They'd agreed to keep an eye out for each other next time they were at Mayday's.

She'd known even then that she would probably never be there again. And she'd bet he suspected as much, too. But last night had been like a time-out from her regular life. A magical moment when her stars had aligned with those of the hottest guy imaginable. And while it was okay to live a little, the way her brother had told her to, she wasn't going to suddenly stop being Cassie Rowe from Idaho.

Last night, she'd felt free to demand what she wanted and give it in return. No compromising. No holding back. Just pure, unadulterated passion that'd fired her up and kept her from worrying about today's flight.

A shiver snaked along her spine. Not much anyway. As the transport bus bounced over a pothole, bringing her closer to her crazy decision to fly into a hurricane-ravaged country, the first buzz of nerves returned.

She pulled the top off her coffee and breathed in the fragrant steam. Definitely a two-cup morning.

Tan, beige and black stone half walls appeared after a few minutes, one with a sign that read United States Coast Guard Air Station Clearwater.

Cassie's mood plummeted as she glimpsed the orange-and-white Jayhawk helicopters in the distance. Guilt bit hard as she remembered how gratefully she'd shaken off her grief last night for those hours of forgetting.

Raeanne, a fellow nurse seated next to her, squeezed her arm.

"I always get such an adrenaline rush at this point."

Cassie nodded, though the only rushing going on inside her was from memories of her brother.

"I was nervous on my first flight, too." Raeanne sipped from her own cup of coffee, her bright Red Cross T-shirt reminding Cassie of their mission. "But everything's done. Our medical supplies are loaded. All we have to do is get on the helicopter."

"Right." Cassie pressed on the corners of her closed eyes with her index fingers. The thought of boarding one—as Jeff had—created a vacuum inside of her, sucking till her chest caved in on itself. She'd wanted closure, but now, confronted with this reality, her wounds all threatened to split open, painful and raw as ever.

At last the bus jerked to a halt and they slumped outside just as the clouds started to drizzle. The members of her emergency team hurried across the dappled tarmac to a white hangar that resembled an Idaho barn, pitched roof and all. The main building had wings, one stretching out to the rear from each end. Surrounding it were orange-and-white planes and helicopters. Uniformed men and women loaded and checked equipment while others saluted before slapping each other on the back.

Their booming laughter did nothing to offset Cassie's rising anxiety. She couldn't help seeing things through Jeff's eyes, remembering how much he'd loved the same kind of close-knit community on his old base. The ground rumbled under her feet as a plane took off. Wind gusted over the slate ocean ruffled with rising waves.

Once this had been Jeff's world. Now it was hers. And as much as that might hurt, where else could she find the understanding that eluded her? The replies she'd gotten to the letters she'd fired off to his commanding officer had lacked the detail she needed.

She worked to school her expression as she followed Raeanne to a group of about ten people—Red

Cross volunteers and Coast Guard servicemen and servicewomen—standing by a flight line, a Jayhawk behind them.

When they reached the circle, she stood by one of the military helicopter's wheels and studied her shoes. The uniforms and aircraft all added to the twist of pain in her chest. For a second, she wished she could run back to that beach where she'd left Mark. But she'd known that living in the moment wasn't always going to be fun.

This day was going to hurt.

"Not everyone's here, but since we're wheels up in ten, we'll go ahead with introductions. I'm Chief Petty Officer Ian McClaughlin, a rescue swimmer and trainer."

Cassie breathed in and out. Focused on steadying herself before she lifted her gaze to the military man still speaking. After Ian McClaughlin shook hands with the leader of Cassie's Red Cross group, a few others in the Jayhawk crew introduced themselves. She strained to focus, but their words swirled around her like the storm outside—background noise for all the other thoughts cramming her head.

Forcing herself to join the conversation, she was preparing to introduce herself when the sound of footsteps penetrated her consciousness.

"Sorry for the holdup, folks." The familiar male voice was like a warm arm around her shoulders, steadying her.

Confused, she turned to see her dark-haired lover from the night before. Except he wasn't naked and whispering sweet words in her ear. He wore a Coast Guard uniform.

And while she'd guessed that Mark was military, she sure never expected he might be part of her transport to Saint Thomas. The shock stole her breath.

"I'm Lieutenant Commander Mark Sampson, pilot with Elizabeth City Air Station." He hadn't spotted her yet as he tipped the black brim of his white hat.

Elizabeth City? That was Jeff's former base.

Suddenly, the air was white around her, burning things away from the edges in. When she took an involuntary sideways step, the nurse next to her murmured some kind of generic encouragement. The woman had no clue that Cassie's brain was short-circuiting, struggling to make sense of Mark being here.

Of Mark being a Jayhawk pilot from Jeff's last station.

"I'm Petty Officer Second Class Larry Volk, flight mechanic with Elizabeth City," continued the introductions.

Cassie couldn't breathe. Fear weighted her shoulders. Dread compounded it.

"Lieutenant Robert Fillmore, copilot with Elizabeth City," spoke up another man.

The whole crew was from North Carolina. What were the odds that this was a group Jeff had known? Jeff had flown with?

Mark was a common enough name. She hadn't thought twice about it last night. But in the context of the Jayhawk and the Elizabeth City connection, she made sense of all the clues. Heard Mark's full name and rank and recalled it listed on the flower arrangement card Jeff's crew had sent when they couldn't attend the memorial. Mark Sampson. The pilot who'd flown her brother's final mission.

The man she'd spent the night with was the same man who had left her brother to drown.

At her strangled exclamation, the pilot's eyes swerved her way, widening in recognition.

But did he really recognize her? Of course not. He had no idea who she was or how deeply she'd betrayed her brother's memory. The thought of it knocked her breath out, like ice water.

Her eyes drifted out of the hangar and back toward the bus. For a moment she envisioned racing to it, returning to the hotel and then to Idaho. But she didn't think she could live with this burden any better there than here. She wasn't that kind of woman any longer.

Hitching her duffel bag higher on her shoulder, she stared at a distant spot over Mark's shoulder. Leaving wouldn't honor her brother. This heartless pilot would not take that from her, too.

No.

She'd go on the mission as planned. Maybe, amid the chaos of this natural disaster, she'd better understand the choices Jeff had made—and the sacrifices. To do that, she'd need to avoid the officer whose presence would be enough to keep her wounds from healing, even if that meant ignoring the strongest attraction she'd ever felt for a man.

WHY WOULDN'T SHE meet his eye?

As introductions rolled on, Mark stared at Cassie and listened to his crazy heartbeat. It'd taken every ounce of willpower to squelch thoughts of their night together during preflight inspection this morning. He'd worried he might never see her again. But here she stood, even more beautiful in natural light, and looking far too vulnerable to fly into the aftermath of a Category 5 storm.

Damn it. He could not let her mess with his head.

Would not let memories of their incredible night distract him from what he really needed. This mission.

And the absolution that each successful operation would bring him.

Exhaust fuel permeated the waterlogged air when more engines fired to life around them. His gaze swept over her as she huddled in the group, her arms crossed, shoulders folding in. The thin, dirty light revealed the purple shadows under her eyes. Shadows he was responsible for.

Did she regret last night? She'd seemed as satisfied as him when they'd parted. Still, the pain he'd noticed in the bar shimmered around her now. Gone was the passionate woman who'd rocked his world.

The redhead beside her finished her introduction and turned, giving the floor to Cassie.

"I'm Cassie Rowe, RN American Red Cross, Greater Idaho," she said, voice ragged. She hit him with a stare like a threat.

"First timer!" proclaimed the woman next to Cassie and a smattering of cheers and claps rose.

"Getting her dollar ride," one of his crew put in.

Rowe. The name backhanded him like a slap from his old man.

Jeff's last name. And hadn't he been from the Midwest? Mark's brain buzzed, his nervous system flashing warnings brighter than any heads-up display on a flight screen. He tried recalling the names he'd written on the card to Jeff's family.

There was definitely a sister.

Outside, the light shower turned into thick, clammy rain. When the group turned his way, he automatically waved them on board, a buzzing in his ears. Time to leave. He had less than five minutes before takeoff. But he had to know.

He tipped his hat to each of the members when they clambered on board, then pulled Cassie aside. She jerked her elbow free and examined him with flat eyes that sucked in everything and emitted nothing.

"Cassie—"

The rain blew against them, shifting, and an engine whined loud as another plane took off.

She put up a hand and backed away, her eyes over-bright. "No. I can't—" She stared around her, dazed, then tossed her duffel bag into the cabin, bounded by him and hauled herself inside the helicopter.

Damn.

"Yo! Time's up, Commander," called Robert through the open cockpit door.

"Got it."

He climbed into his seat, donned his helmet and strapped himself in. Robert shot Mark a questioning look, which he ignored as he compartmentalized and began the familiar start-up routines. Didn't Cassie's last name trip a signal in anyone else's mind from his crew? His hand fisted in his lap while Robert moved the battery switch to On, flipped on the APU and checked through the hydraulic systems. Mark fired up the engines and the rotors whirred to life, the blades slicing through the fog rolling in off the bay.

After cross-checking his engine and system instruments against his start checklist, he tuned up the ground frequency and waited for a break in the chatter to request taxi clearance.

Something skimmed across Mark's mind. Cassie's eyes. Same color as Jeff's. Then there was his old crewmate's leave request for a sister graduating nursing school.

Cold sweat popped on his brow.

Shit.

"She's Jeff's sister," he murmured under his breath, his voice ragged.

His shoulders tightened. Not the right time to dwell on this. But holy hell. Given her reaction, she'd realized who he was, too.

Her parents blamed him for Jeff's death. No doubt Cassie did, as well.

And how could he fault her? He hadn't stopped blaming himself.

He squeezed his eyes shut, blocking out the riot of thought and focused, drawing on his training. He was supposed to be putting this shit behind him. He'd sworn up and down to the military docs that he could handle flying.

That meant he would damn well get this bird in the air and put the mission first.

When the ground control conversation ended, he slowed his breathing. "St. Pete ground, Coast Guard 6039, IFR Clearance on request."

The controller's voice sounded through his headset. "Roger, Coast Guard 6039. Stand by."

While Mark waited for final verification of his international flight plan, he continued down his checklist, the clipboard balanced on his knees.

After a minute, his headphones crackled. "Coast

Guard 6039, St. Pete ground. Cleared to the Nassau MYNN Airport as filed. On departure fly heading three-five-zero, climb and maintain sixteen hundred feet, expect three thousand ten minutes after departure. Departure frequency 121.5. Squawk 0105."

Mark nodded to Rob, who jotted down the information as Mark repeated it verbatim to the controller.

"Read back correct. Advise when ready for taxi," the controller replied then tuned out.

After ticking off the last item on his checklist, Mark returned to the top and verified it all again. This liftoff would be textbook; Cassie wouldn't rattle him.

Rob pointed at the timer, moved his finger in a clockwise motion and raised an eyebrow. Right. Too much delay. Mark slipped the board by the side of his seat and called on the designated frequency.

"St. Pete ground, Coast Guard 6039 at the Coast Guard ramp with information Alpha, IFR to Nassau, ready to taxi."

Rain streaked down the helicopter's windshield and the air inside the narrow cockpit was humid. Despite his turning up the ventilation, sweat pooled at the base of his neck and trickled down his back.

"Roger, Coast Guard 6039. Taxi through the back door to Runway 36L, hold short at Alpha."

Mark pulled up the collective and pushed forward on the cyclic. When they reached five miles per hour, he pressed on the brake and the helicopter jerked to a quick, satisfying halt.

He accelerated again, hoping he hadn't scared anyone with the brake check. Hadn't flustered Cassie. "Everyone all set in back?" he asked into his mic through the ICS. An image of Cassie buckled into one of the seats twisted his gut. Jeff had sat back there once, too, secure and certain of his safety, a brother of the fin— as the air and sea rescuers called themselves—family, yet Mark had let him down.

Technically, a weakened cable and low fuel had been blamed for the accident, but Mark knew better. Most nights when he closed his eyes the fatal incident played out in vivid detail, making sleep impossible. It was why he'd been at the bar last night. Why he'd told Cassie he wouldn't make for good company.

A year ago he'd been at the peak of his career. An aircraft commander, instructor pilot, flight examiner, and decorated search and rescue pilot with a spotless record. A man who embodied his profession's motto: "So others may live." After he'd been forced to make a decision that had cost a crew member's life, however, his faith in himself had been shattered.

For most of his life, he'd strived to differentiate himself from his incarcerated father. To prove that he could be one of the good guys. He'd joined the Coast Guard to become that hero, to save others. Some hero he'd turned out to be. Losing a member of his crew had wrecked him.

He'd come back to justify the military's faith in him. To prove himself again.

"Roger, Commander." Larry's response sounded in his ear after some static, the loud whirring snuffing out every other sound.

The Jayhawk's wheels rolled smoothly as he taxied to the runway, halted on the hold short line and tuned into the designated channel.

"St. Pete tower, Coast Guard 6039, hold short Alpha."

"Coast Guard 6039, position and hold. Waiting for traffic to clear."

Mark watched a Herc roll ahead of him, the long-range surveillance plane's four propellers whirling. The HC-130H was the oldest model in the fleet, but rescue ready and part of the massive response Clearwater mounted for the storm's aftermath now that it was safe to approach. Would it perform as expected? Would he?

"Position and hold Runway 36L," Mark barked into the mic. "Coast Guard copter 6039. Request for hover check."

"Roger, 6039. Cleared for hover check. Advise when ready for takeoff."

They rose ten feet and Mark scrutinized the instruments: 88 percent torque, 100 percent Nr, 2–3 degrees nose up altitude, 4–5 degrees left wing down and all other systems in the green. So far so good. Once stabilized, he checked for proper flight control response and verified his power setting. Nothing was wrong, yet he felt off.

Rob opened a bag of Jolly Ranchers and held it out. "Want some?"

"Nah." Mark lowered the helicopter. His eyes fixed on the ground, mind focused on a precise landing position. Not on Cassie. Not Jeff. He brushed at the moisture beading his forehead.

"You okay?"

"Fine," he said, his voice firm.

And he was. Had to be. He shook some of the pieces into his hand after all and tossed back a couple.

He'd worried this first large-scale disaster response since Jeff's loss would shake loose old insecurities. Challenge his hard-won equilibrium. But he'd arrived on the flight line clearheaded for the first time in months. What an irony that Cassie Rowe had been responsible for that. She'd leveled him out better than any of the mandatory visits with a base shrink—had made him feel normal again. Until she'd sent him straight back to hell.

When the Herc disappeared from view, Mark cleared his throat. "Coast Guard 6039, ready for take-off."

He gave Rob a thumbs-up. Simultaneously, he pulled the collective to 98 percent torque, adjusted the tail rotor pedals to maintain heading and maneuvered the cyclic to stay centerline. As they rose slowly, he transitioned to forward flight.

"6039 airborne." As they gained altitude, Mark turned to heading three hundred fifty and continued with his departure procedures, the helicopter shuddering slightly before smoothing out. The Sikorsky shuffle.

A normal takeoff, just like always. Nothing wrong. And nothing would go wrong on this mission, he vowed, then loosened his white-knuckle grip on the stick. The gray sprawl of ocean appeared below as Mark's gaze drifted to the MFD screen. Current weather images of the hurricane continuously updated in the newly installed test weather radar. Although the hurricane had jogged east, a few bands still streaked across southern Florida.

He verified the correct course set for the Nassau, where they'd refuel before going on to the mission's staging area in the Virgin Islands, and slumped back in his seat, his joints stiff. He had to get over this jittery sense that something wasn't right.

Cassie's accusing expression swam into view. She had every right to hate him. It'd been a long time before he'd been able to face himself in the mirror.

So why had she joined such a treacherous mission? This was her first disaster operation. At least Jeff had been trained for what he faced. Cassie had little preparation for this scale of an emergency and his protective instincts rose. He'd failed her brother and wouldn't let another Rowe family member come to harm on his watch. He owed Jeff that much and more.

But aside from that obligation, he would put Cassie Rowe out of his head. He'd fought too hard to get back in the cockpit after the weeks he'd been grounded following Jeff's death. No way would he let a woman get to him, undermine all he'd devoted his life to achieve.

Fat splats of rain peppered the glass and he glanced down at his radar. The last vestiges of the hurricane brewed their mischief up ahead. The final salvo in a storm that had inflicted devastating damage…yet a certain blonde on board his aircraft felt like the greater threat.

He would not be with her again, even if she'd had any inclination to come near him a second time. Getting close to Cassie would jeopardize the mission. His career. Possibly his sanity.

The problem with playing with this particular fire, however, was already knowing how sweet the burn would be.

4

"Good work, Nurse Rowe." The Red Cross's chief nurse, Marjorie Little, nodded briskly as she strode down the long row of cots lining the temporary aid station's sides.

They'd erected the house-size tent this morning since the inflatable field hospital units wouldn't be operational for a couple of days. Minimum.

"Thanks." Cassie peeled her damp collar from her neck and hoped for sooner than later. She secured an ACE wrap around her latest patient's swollen ankle and turned, striving not to sway on her feet. It'd been a long ten-hour shift, but damned if she'd let it show. In fact, strange as it sounded, she'd enjoyed the frenetic pace. It was so different than the usual crawl of taking blood pressure and giving flu vaccinations at her father's general practice. Best of all, she'd been too busy to think of a certain pilot…

Moans and cries, accompanied by murmuring medical volunteers and beeping, generator-fueled machines, comprised the day's sound track, as relentless as the pelting rain against their canvas roof. The combined scents of sweat and antiseptic hung in the humid air. It coated her mouth, lined her nasal passages. She could smell it on her uniform. Her hair even...

"It's all gone," sobbed her patient, Melinda, an island tour guide. She clutched a small framed photo of her family—the only thing she'd managed to grab before her house collapsed, she'd told Cassie earlier.

"I'm so sorry." She clamped down her own fatigue and smoothed a hand over her charge's forehead. Good. Cooler. The ibuprofen had kicked in.

Despite her relief, a restless feeling swept through her. For the hundredth time today, she wished she could do more to help. Her patient would regain her health, but what about the rest of her life?

The flattened structures she'd glimpsed before landing on a less damaged coastal section being used for the Coast Guard's staging area flashed through her mind. Eroded beaches, boats and debris appeared to be shoved ashore by an invisible, monstrous hand. The same one that'd punched out windows and torn the roofs off the few standing buildings. Lives, ripped apart at the seams, crushed and pulverized by powers beyond their control.

Although she had never experienced anything like that, in her own way, she could relate.

Her weary gaze drifted over the large bandage that hid a stitched gash on the woman's temple.

She stiffened.

Right.

Tetanus shot.

Her patient risked lockjaw.

Adrenaline zipped through Cassie. A buzz. Urgent and fierce.

She moved aside as Raeanne slid by to attend to a writhing man on the cot beside Melinda's and flagged down a physician.

"Doctor." Cassie held out her patient's paperwork. "I need a signature for a tetanus shot order."

The stooped man scanned the patient's file, peeked at her bandage and scrawled something fairly illegible on the chart before hurrying on.

"Do you have any allergies?" she asked her charge while consulting the chart. It never hurt to double-check. Melinda shook her head.

"I'll be back in a few minutes, Taufik." Raeanne squeezed Cassie's arm as she passed by again, her faint smile appearing and disappearing as fast as it came.

"Any chance you might be pregnant?" Cassie continued.

"No."

She snapped the chart closed and gave Melinda a reassuring smile. "I'll be right back with your shot."

A moment later, she slipped behind the curtained partition that held their medication and other supplies.

"How's it going?" asked Raeanne, tapping a couple of oxys into a paper cup.

"Good." She scanned the syringes, looking for the right size. She selected the correct needle and turned slowly, stabbing pain shooting down her spine.

"Good?" Raeanne dropped the bottle in the med cabinet, locked it and blew a dangling red curl out of her face. Her narrowed green eyes skimmed over Cassie. "That almost sounded like you meant it. You were so quiet on the flight, I thought you were having second thoughts."

And she had been, she mused, grabbing a vial of

Dtap. "I'm glad I came." Which was mostly true, if not for Mark.

Still, she couldn't shake the memory of how his arms had made her feel safe, his kisses transporting her away from all the fear of the upcoming mission. Little had she known he was a devil in disguise.

And now she risked seeing him again when she retrieved the bag she'd left on his helicopter. If only she'd taken a moment to remember her things rather than dashing away the second they landed, desperate to avoid Mark.

At her frustrated breath, Raeanne raised her eyebrows. "Now you definitely don't sound sincere. Spill it, girl. You're allowed to complain on your first day. After that, I'll only pretend to listen."

Cassie's mood lifted and she smiled, or tried to. Her lips felt too tired to move. "I'm no whiner."

The curtains parted and a couple of nurses hustled inside. "I need coffee. Stat," rasped one of them, a woman with thick dark hair done up in a topknot. She yanked off her stained uniform top and grabbed another from the shelf.

"Me, too." Her companion popped in a piece of gum before grabbing an armload of fresh linens. "When is our relief coming on?"

"Two hours," Raeanne put in. "A minute over that, we strike."

She stared at the chortling group before laughing, too, marveling at the nurses' capacity for humor in the face of grueling work. It was a coping mechanism for sure, and a way to bond. Never before had she felt such camaraderie. She liked it.

Was this what had appealed to Jeff? Tempted him

to work such a risky job? She'd always thought he was crazy. Had wished he'd stop giving their anxiety-prone mother reasons to fret. But now she saw it. A glimmer, maybe, of what had motivated him to leave their hometown.

Why he'd urged her to do the same.

"So, who knows something about our hot pilot?" one of the nurses asked. The strong smell of antiseptic soap stung Cassie's nose as the bubbly brunette lathered suds across her palms and beneath her fingernails.

She pulled in 0.5 ml of Dtap and capped her needle with shaking hands.

"He lost one of his crew members," Raeanne supplied. Large bubbles glugged from the water dispenser as she pulled its blue lever. "Really broke him up. He was grounded, too. Had to get clearance to fly again. My cousin, Rob, the copilot, said this is the first disaster relief mission LCDR Sampson's flown since then. They're all a little worried for him."

The other RN ripped a couple of paper towels from the dispenser and turned. She arched a brow. "I'll comfort him."

"Why are four of my nurses not treating patients?" snapped the chief nurse, breaking up the tableau by thrusting through the curtain, her mouth pressed in a firm line.

"Sorry, Nurse Little," gasped the brunette.

"Just getting medication." Raeanne shook one of her cups, making the pills rattle.

"And gossiping," asserted Nurse Little. "One, we don't spread rumors." She ticked her fingers. "Two, we don't waste precious time doing so when there are patients to treat. Am I clear?"

"Yes, ma'am," whispered the cowed young women as they scurried back into the main part of the tent.

Cassie, however, didn't trust her trembling legs to move so she held on to the plastic shelving, hoping the spinning world would stop soon.

Mark had been grounded?

This was his first disaster mission since Jeff's disappearance?

She pictured his dark expression last night when they'd met. Recalled his assurance that he wasn't the best company. Had his concern for this trip been the reason?

Yet it didn't match the image she'd formed of the pilot who'd abandoned Jeff. The overconfident, callous man who cared only about following procedures, not saving lives.

The rumors had to be wrong.

"Cassie, you look pale."

She shook her head, so many thoughts buzzing in her brain she couldn't speak one out loud.

"Yes, you are. And tired." A firm hand pressed against her brow and Nurse Little's eyes bored into hers. "This is your first mission, correct?"

She nodded. Beyond the curtains someone shrieked, a long, agonizing sound that trailed off ominously.

"And you've been working…"

"Since we arrived, ma'am," she murmured, dredging her voice from its hiding spot, somewhere down deep in her throat. She wasn't about to mention that she hadn't slept the night before, too busy tangling limbs with the helicopter pilot responsible for her brother's death.

"Right." Nurse Little took the tetanus needle from

Cassie's hand. "I'm relieving you tonight. Give me a report on your patients, then shower and bed. I'll need you back at 0600 hours. That's an order."

"But Melinda…" protested Cassie. And it was her turn for a new admit. The screaming patient…that had to be hers. She was needed. Couldn't quit now.

"I'll give her the shot. Tetanus?"

"Yes. But really, I can…"

Nurse Little arched an eyebrow. "I believe I'm perfectly capable of giving a shot. And a directive. Is there some other issue I'm unaware of?"

Cassie hung her head. "I left my duffel on the helicopter. I don't have anything to change into."

Nurse Little pointed at a bag in the corner. "You can borrow a clean T-shirt and shorts from me. Anything else?"

Cassie backed up. "No, ma'am."

Her supervisor's face softened. "Get some rest, dear. Lord knows we'll need a fresh pair of hands in the morning."

"Thank you." After reporting out to her superior, she grabbed the clothes and headed through the back entrance to the hastily built women's showers—basically a couple of stalls with sheets for curtains and a self-pumping water unit.

Despite the crude setup, she sighed when she stripped off her limp uniform and lathered her hair, washing the grime away, wishing the devastating losses she'd witnessed today were as easy to erase. None of the wounds she'd treated had come close to soothing the hurts of these people who'd been separated from homes and loved ones.

She pictured the desperate locals who'd searched

the patient board, looking for their family members, leaving hollow eyed and empty-handed. How she ached for them. She knew what loss felt like. The crushing pressure that seemed to bury your heart alive, made taking a full breath impossible, your mind spinning in hopeless circles, trying and failing to understand that a part of you was gone forever. That your life would never be the same, would never be whole.

Water pulsed against her hair as she scraped her nails over her scalp, massaging in the shampoo. Pushing back the rising darkness, Cassie drew on a memory of the most rewarding part of the day—reuniting a girl with a stuffed dog that had been a dumb-luck find. Cassie had spotted it during her lunch break when she'd helped pull one of the stretchers off an emergency vehicle.

How elated she'd felt to see the girl's tears dry and a small smile emerge. The ultimate rewards weren't always big successes, but sometimes the quiet, small victories.

She turned beneath the water and held out the length of her hair. Shampoo streamed to the drain and swirled, rising in bubbles before disappearing. Washcloth in hand, she rubbed a bar of brown soap then slid the cleanser over her body, the stringent smell stinging her nose. Despite the devastation caused by the storm, or perhaps because of it, Cassie had most often witnessed love today. Dedicated spouses, partners and family members, waiting for hours outside the station, patiently holding vigil until their loved one was out of danger.

Love…

She'd never been in love before. Commuting to her

local college, then moving into the apartment above her parents' garage, meant she hadn't gotten out much. Dated. Definitely no mind-blowing one-night stands like last night.

Heat flared at the juncture of her thighs as she skimmed the wash cloth there, her flesh deliciously sore after the long, passionate night.

If Mark was anyone else, she would have said it was the greatest sex of her life. When was the last time she'd felt so giddy and uninhibited? So powerful?

Only it'd been a lie. A cruel cosmic joke that made her want to scream, not laugh. Mark was her enemy.

Yet, based on Raeanne's story, she wondered.

Did Jeff haunt Mark, too?

An alarm sounded as she finished rinsing. Warned that such a signal heralded increased wind and dangerous conditions, she yanked the T-shirt over her slick body, pulled on the shorts and dashed outside.

Straight into a wall of muscle.

"Oh. Excuse me," she muttered, her apology withering on her lips as she glanced up. Mark.

Her pulse quickened under his intent stare, shock rooting her feet to the ground. The gaining wind whipped her wet hair around her face.

His gaze traveled down her body, from the collar of her wet shirt to the hem of Nurse Little's shorts, which, thanks to Cassie's longer frame, barely covered her ass. His predatory eyes narrowed.

Before she could whirl away, she caught sight of her duffel, dangling from his hand.

"That's mine."

He cleared his throat. "I was dropping it at the aid station. Didn't think you'd still be working."

Oh. So he'd hoped to avoid her? Anger sizzled through her, despite her own strategy to evade him.

Well. Too bad, flyboy.

"And why's that?" she demanded, grabbing the bag from him. At the brush of his fingers against hers, hungry need growled low in her gut and she shoved it down. Focused on her anger. Outrage. "You didn't think I'd last?"

Before he could answer, something whizzed by her ear and he grabbed her, lightning fast, and pulled them to the ground. Her heartbeat pounded in her ears as he crouched over her protectively, his smell familiar and sexy as hell.

She shoved him away. "I don't need your help," she muttered then stopped. Her mouth dropped open at the sight of a piece of sheet metal buried in the shower wall where she'd stood seconds ago.

The words *thank you* could never come out of her mouth when it came to Mark...yet he'd just saved her. Conflicting emotions churned in her stomach like the lousy coffee she'd drunk all day—gratitude, fury and desire.

God help her.

"I'm getting you back to your quarters," he said in a tone she'd bet was usually obeyed. He shrugged out of his uniform jacket, draped it around her shoulders and hustled her toward the nearby women's quarters.

OF ALL THE people to run into after his long day. Cassie Rowe.

The last person he wanted to see.

Mark had struggled to compartmentalize as he'd worked to rescue survivors. Flying through bands of the storm, he'd sweated ten gallons trying to wrestle the Jayhawk through the remnants of the hurricane weather, pulling people out of tossing waves. That used to all be in a day's work. Now? He battled demons harder than the buffeting winds, Jeff's specter riding shotgun beside him, a dark copilot and a reminder of the biggest screwup of Mark's career.

He needed some R & R to decompress. Get his shit together. He was flight ready, damn it. Could more than handle this disaster response.

As for Cassie?

He had to get his feelings for her under control, too. His plan to leave her bag with the Red Cross's chief nurse would have helped. Out of sight, out of mind.

Then, holy hell.

When she'd dashed out of the showers, a flimsy T-shirt molded to her voluptuous breasts, short shorts revealing the sweet curve of her ass, all the blood in his brain had gone south. In an instant, he'd forgotten all the reasons he was staying away from her, his hands itching to touch her smooth skin long before his sense kicked in.

He took a deep breath and tried to banish the image of a nearly naked Cassie from his mind. The oversize jacket that hung to her knees should have helped…but he kept picturing her gorgeous body on the beach last night. The feel of her soft flesh, yielding to him. Demanding, too.

He quickened his pace.

"Hey!" she protested, flipping back her damp hair. All around them, the air moved like a wild thing, dark and dangerous, reminding him of everything he'd battled at the controls today over the Atlantic. How close he'd come to losing the bubble.

He needed her out of here. She drew his attention like a fireworks display. One about to detonate in his face.

"Slow down or let go," she warned him, edging out of his grip.

Which was just as well. He had no business putting his hands on her.

"You didn't have a problem keeping up last night." Where had that come from? He sounded like a horny teenager. Or an arrogant asshole.

She huffed beside him as a downed palm tree frond caught against the coat and she yanked a piece of stray foliage loose, her shape barely discernable now in the moonless night. "Really?"

He slowed his gait, guiding them carefully over the branches. "That's my recollection."

"I'd rather forget. I wish it'd never happened."

Her bitter tone left little doubt that she meant every word.

So why wasn't he glad about that?

"If I'd known..." he began.

A bitter laugh escaped her. "Then what? You would have avoided me. Stayed away like you did at Jeff's memorial?"

"An emergency came up."

"You could have visited his stone anytime."

Guilt ripped through him. Yes. He'd thought of that. Was planning to go, actually, after this mission. After he'd figured out what the hell to say to Jeff's family. But now Cassie was here, her presence more intimate than he could ever have prepared for, catching him flat-footed.

He breathed in the bracing, briny air. "Look, I can't take back what happened last night."

"That's it, isn't it? You can't take back any of it. So what's the point? I've got my bag so you can go now. I'll find my way alone." She wrapped the coat tighter around herself. Was she still oblivious to the flying debris, or just that stubborn?

"Where's your room?" he challenged as he ducked beneath a tree, and pulled her with him when the air suddenly swooshed by carrying stinging pebbles.

Her eyes darted around him. "I'm number ten."

He raised an eyebrow. "And where is that?"

She flung an arm east. "There?" She pivoted and peered into the night. "Or did Raeanne say to the left of the showers…?"

Overhead, a Jayhawk whirred, going out to sea. Out to face the nightmare winds that he'd just waged war with for hours.

He nodded firmly. Felt his back teeth clench. "Right. Let's go." The USCG and Red Cross had commandeered a resort that had suffered limited damage for their operations. He'd passed the side they'd designated as women's quarters on his way here—a string of bungalows deemed safe by the engineering crew.

"Just tell me where…"

Despite the gloom, her blond hair gleamed, her fresh-scrubbed face making her look young. Vulnerable. Why the hell had she come here? Anger seared his insides. She should be home safe with her family. Not in a place still full of danger. Where she could get hurt, like Jeff. Where she added to the crap factor of his first mission back.

"I want to make sure you get there." That was all this was. Duty. Nothing more. He owed Jeff a debt, and her presence here couldn't have been a stronger reminder.

She kicked a car part out of her path. A tailpipe. "Shouldn't you be more concerned with your pilot duties? You must have other people to keep safe."

Her words slashed right through his chest. When she jerked away, he didn't stop her.

Suddenly she slowed. Swung around. The wind lifted her hair so that it swirled like a veil. "Forget I said that. We're almost there anyhow."

She fell into step with him again and silence stretched between them, taut, nearly to its breaking point.

"Why are you here?" he asked at last, wanting an answer to the question that'd plagued him since he'd learned her identity. If he understood that, he'd leave her alone, he vowed.

Then, without warning, the wind blew itself out for a long moment, the warm air seeming to hold its breath. They paused beside an overhang and the rushing ocean nipped at the jagged beach below.

She looked out at the sea. "I want to know what happened to my brother," she murmured quietly.

"Everything is in the report," he forced himself to say, moved by her words.

Not everything, whispered a voice inside, one he smothered. He wouldn't listen to it. Relive it. Much too dangerous.

"But I don't *know*." She turned and her anguished eyes met his.

"There's nothing more I can share," he said curtly and ignored the scalding regret that flared in his gut when her mouth trembled. Her face was an accusation.

"Of course not," she said, her voice cracking. "That's all it is with you guys. Files. Records. Procedures. But what about people?" She jabbed a finger into his chest "What about Jeff?"

"Jeff was a brave man. The best rescue swimmer I ever had the honor to work with."

They were the truest words he'd ever spoken but not the whole truth. Not even close.

"Yet you left him to die." Her mouth thinned.

Words slammed against the lump in his throat. Collided with one another, forming a pile that made it hard to breathe.

He couldn't go any further in this conversation or he'd risk falling back down the black hole that'd kept him out of the cockpit. He'd worked hard to fly again and needed to be in control...in command.

"Your quarters are over there." He pointed at the bungalows a few yards away and pinned his gaze on a distant spot over her shoulder.

After a moment, she made a strangled noise and stomped away, leaving him alone in the dark.

He watched until she slipped inside her room. Cassie's desperate words returned to him on the wind. *Yet you left him to die.*

He had left Jeff to die.

And he'd never forgive himself. He didn't deserve anything, but he needed the absolution the rigorous work in the days ahead could give him.

And he'd do everything in his power to make sure none of those days included Cassie.

5

CASSIE RUBBED HER aching back and trudged outside the aid station the next evening, heading home. The overcast sky grayed the uneven terrain and her boots squelched in ankle-deep mud more than once before she remembered to keep her weary eyes on the ground.

Twelve hours. Where had the time gone? It seemed like she'd started her day shift only moments ago, tired but determined to banish the thoughts of Mark that'd plagued her all night.

Was he in the air now?

She scanned the empty sky, its steady drizzle streaming down her face, dripping from her chin. The air held the salt tang of the sea.

Gulls wheeled and shrieked, then dove back to the ocean, out of the persistent wind. Whitecaps striped the churning water while palm trees bent with each salted gust. The massive Category 5 hurricane had stalled east and its bands continued to lash the precarious island. From the nonstop line of patients, it seemed few of the residents had escaped unscathed. The injured and ill list kept growing.

She should feel disheartened. Discouraged even.

Strange that this urgent, unpredictable work left her feeling fulfilled instead. Stressed? Yes, of course. Yet it also settled a restless part of her nature she hadn't known existed, or admitted to herself, until now.

Did that make sense?

No.

She was tired and probably—definitely—not thinking straight.

But deep down, something about being here felt right.

It had been twelve months since Jeff's death, and she'd spent half that time incapacitated by grief. Now, for the first time, she'd had a day where she'd thought of him often but in a good way.

While treating patients, she'd pictured him alongside her, flashing the wide smile he wore when lending a hand to others. He would have enjoyed this work.

The familiar US Coast Guard patch, attached to a duffel in the back of a parked military SUV, caught her eye and she stopped to study it. A blue eagle, wings spread, dominated the center, an embroidered American flag across its chest. She mouthed the Latin words beneath the emblem. *"Semper Paratus."*

Always ready.

Yes. That had been Jeff.

She pushed back her flimsy hood as the rain eased and fog rolled off the ocean, thickening the air to murk.

When a cat strutted over and arched its spine, Cassie crouched to stroke its back. Wet fur clumped around its narrow face and one of its oversize ears bent at the tip.

"Hey, beauty," she murmured. The cat pressed its cheek into Cassie's hand and purred. "Who do you belong to?" Before she could check for a name tag, the cat bolted away, swallowed by the thickening mist.

Cassie followed it a few steps then stopped. It'd be impossible to catch given the worsening visibility. In fact... Cassie turned in a slow circle. She no longer had her bearings. Which way was home? Taking her best guess, she headed in what she hoped was the right direction. She couldn't wait to close her stinging eyes.

At least her whirlwind day kept her from focusing on the enigmatic pilot who'd left her yesterday with more questions than answers.

The most haunting one of all...was he struggling with Jeff's loss as much as she?

Off in the distance, the sea smashed against the beach, relentless and powerful. Cassie shrugged off her jacket now that the rain seemed well and truly gone. In its place, the cloudy, humid air clung to her skin, a clammy layer, thin and sticky as cellophane.

When Raeanne had mentioned Mark's suffering yesterday, Cassie had dismissed it. After watching him struggle to contain his emotions, however, something inside her had shifted. Her antagonism had tempered. And in spite of everything, some of that connection she'd felt to him on the beach that first night had returned.

She'd wanted to know, not just what'd happened to Jeff, but what'd happened to Mark, too.

That need to understand him made no sense when he'd made it clear he wanted nothing more to do with her. When she shouldn't want a damn thing to do with him, either. Her family would disown her if they knew about her time with the pilot they blamed for Jeff's death.

"Help!" came a hoarse shout in the distance. A man's voice.

Cassie cupped her hands around her mouth and called, "Hello?" Her eyes strained in the gathering dark and fog, making out the shapes of overturned cars, downed power lines and a debris-filled roadway, the remains of one-story buildings leaning on either side. A putrid stench rose around her and she coughed. She must have wandered off the resort.

"Hello?" she tried again.

"Here!" An elderly man emerged from the gloom. His dark eyes darted to hers and he beckoned to the damaged house behind him. "Please! Help my wife. She's fainted."

Cassie bolted after him, across a yard made of something crunchy—seashells and pebbles. She hurried into a mostly upright house and paused, letting her eyes adjust to pitch dark.

"I'm Cassie. A nurse. Where's your wife, sir?"

The old man leaned against a table and wheezed, "In bedroom. There. Her name. It is Eloise. I am Jacque. We celebrate fiftieth anniversary here."

What a terrible holiday. She wouldn't let it end in tragedy.

Following Jacque's point, she entered a narrow bedroom, the man a step behind her. A thin woman lay prone on the wood floor. Her eyes fluttered slowly and her chest rose as she gasped for air. Cassie dropped to her knees and pressed her fingers to the side of the woman's throat.

An erratic pulse.

Worse, a thready one.

"Eloise? I'm a nurse here to help you. Can you hear me?"

The woman's mouth sagged open slightly and a strangled sound escaped her.

"What happened?" she asked Jacque as she ran her hands over Eloise, checking for injuries. Cassie's shirt clung to her drenched skin. Sweat rolled down her cheeks and dripped onto her collarbone.

Jacque passed trembling fingers over his wrinkled brow. "We forgot passports when we evacuate. We come back for them. Eloise had the—ah, how do you say—burn in her belly and neck? She said not to worry, but it get worse. Then she fell." He dropped his face in his hands and his shoulders shook.

"Jacque. I need you to stay calm. For Eloise." She fished a penlight from her pocket, opened the woman's mouth and checked her airway. Open.

"Her stomach and throat burning is acid reflux," she continued, thinking out loud... Was the woman hypoglycemic? Epileptic? Reflux didn't cause you to faint...affect your heart...unless—

Her head snapped up. "Does your wife have a history of heart disease?"

Jacque cocked his head, his expression blank.

She pressed her hand to her chest. "Heart. Does your wife have heart problems?"

"No. She is always healthy." Jacque stared down at his wife, his features stiff.

"Has she had chest pain recently?" She pressed on Eloise's fingers, observing capillary refill time.

He shook his head and pulled out a pocket handkerchief. After blowing his nose, he said, "Her teeth. All of them. On this side. They hurt. We need a dentist."

"So the whole jaw. Not just one tooth?" Her hunch might be right.

Please let it be wrong.

He nodded and his dense white eyebrows crashed together. "I don't understand."

"I think I do," she said, dread drumming deep in her gut.

Acid reflux. Referred jaw pain. Shortness of breath. Diaphoresis. Classic symptoms of a heart attack in women, and often fatally misdiagnosed. She needed EMTs, an AED machine, nitro. Now.

"Hang in there, Eloise," she whispered in her patient's ear. After giving her limp hand a reassuring squeeze, she shoved to her feet. "I'll be right back."

"No!" called Jacque, his voice strained. How long had the poor man been calling for help?

She pivoted at the doorway "I'll be right back with help. In the meantime, keep talking to Eloise. She's going to get through this."

Sprinting out the door, she skidded onto the street.

She cupped her hands around her mouth and screamed for help. White air whirled around her as she turned in circles. Tamping down her panic, she could barely see her fingers. How would she find her way back to the resort and Red Cross station when she didn't know which way it was?

An innocent woman's life hung in the balance. She damn well needed to find help. Fast.

"SHE LEFT THE station thirty minutes ago and never came home."

Raeanne's words rang in Mark's ears as he veered off the second track he'd tried since the nurse ran into him, worried about Cassie.

His pulse thudded in his temples and his harsh

breaths burned in his lungs. He'd sworn to protect Cassie and needed to find her. Fast.

Dangerous possibilities clawed at his brain, shredding his thoughts as he imagined her wandering the storm-ravaged island alone.

"Help!"

Mark jerked to a stop. Strained to listen. Cassie?

"Coming!" he hollered. "Keep yelling so I can follow your voice."

"What?" She sounded closer; he swerved left and forward.

"It's Mark." His boots crunched over the debris clogging the road.

"Mark?" she called, louder still, and he zeroed in on her location.

"Yes! Stay put. Don't move!" he ordered, his heart thudding hard enough to break a rib.

And then he spied her.

Blond hair fell around her gorgeous face, her large eyes doing something funny to his gut.

"What are you doing out here?" He grabbed her, rougher than he should have. But a fierce need to feel her whole and safe in his arms seized him. Short-circuited his brain. He dropped his cheek to the top of her head, breathing in her honey-vanilla scent for a split second.

"I've got a female heart attack vic in her late sixties, early seventies. Name's Eloise. She's in bradycardia and respiratory distress."

Mark yanked out his radio and called for assistance as he hustled after Cassie. Inside the precarious-looking house, he got right down to business. He knelt beside the alarmingly still woman.

"Eloise. Can you hear me?" He gently shook the

victim's shoulder. He took her pulse and listened for respiration. A massive heart attack. Fatal possibly. His pulse quickened as he tamped down on his emotions and got ready to work.

Go time.

A man on the other side of the victim leaned over, his face nearly as gray as his spouse's. "Eloise. *Pouvez-vous m'entendre, mon amour?*"

"She's not breathing," Mark reported in the brisk voice he used in urgent, dire situations. It instilled calm. Got people moving.

He glanced at a determined-looking Cassie, who quickly moved to Eloise's head, saying, "Begin chest compressions."

He nodded, laced his fingers, locked his elbows and pressed down. When he'd finished his first set of thirty, Cassie tilted Eloise's chin, pinched her nose and blew twice into her mouth before listening for a resumption of respiration.

He held his own breath as he studied her, looking for a sign they'd revived the woman, though it was unlikely this early on. At last, Cassie straightened and shook her head. Other than a small line appearing between her brows, she looked calm. Prepared. Ready.

Four more rounds of CPR and suddenly the woman's eyelashes fluttered. A faint rasp emerged from her throat.

"Patient breathing," Cassie announced with her ear beside Eloise's mouth.

Cautious optimism built. He'd seen too many of these situations go south to give hope free rein just yet.

He sat back on his heels and snatched up the woman's wrist. "Pulse has returned. Rate—" he paused, glancing at his watch "—thirty beats per minute. Patient still in bradycardia. Arrhythmia."

Cassie nodded and he marveled at the steely set to her chin, the determined glint in her eye. Here was another side to the passionate woman who'd rocked his world then turned it upside down.

"Veuillez, mon amour. S'il vous plaît," sobbed their victim's husband and his sympathy went out to the guy.

Suddenly, EMTs rushed into the room, along with Dylan, the crew member he'd radioed. Cassie stepped aside with him as the medics hooked the woman up to an AED. After a couple of jolts, the team deemed her stable enough to move and the entire group hustled from the home, Dylan guiding out the hysterical husband.

"We did it." Cassie spoke behind him as he watched the departing emergency crew.

He turned and gazed down at her pale face. Even with her hair mussed and her eyes shadowed, she was still kick-ass beautiful and the sexiest woman he'd ever seen.

And damn capable, too. Her steady, levelheaded emergency response earned his appreciation and respect.

Unable to resist, he picked up a lock of her hair and let it slide through his fingers. His voice was a soft growl. "I'm glad I found you."

Her gorgeous eyes met his, questioning. "Were you looking for me?"

He nodded, his tongue thick and heavy in his mouth. It was their first civil exchange since the night they met and it felt good. "Raeanne, too. She told me you hadn't come home after your shift."

She leaned her cheek against his hand for a moment then extricated herself and headed for the door. "He really loves her. Did you see his face when Eloise came back?"

He studied her for a moment, reminded that Cassie was a small-town girl with values to match. She was only here out of the goodness of her heart and then she'd be gone again. He had no more business spending what felt like stolen time with her now than he had the night they met.

"Yes," he said gruffly. He cupped her elbow and steered her back into the street, their feet stirring the dissipating fog.

An awkward silence swelled as they picked their way to the side entrance to the resort and its bungalows. The night was damp and still and the air heavy with moisture. Seagulls perched along roof lines, the only other signs of life on the empty streets.

Love.

With a father in jail and a mother too busy working three jobs to date, he'd only ever witnessed devotion like that once before. The commander who'd mentored Mark, Frank Gilford. He'd married his high school sweetheart and never left on a mission without telling her that he loved her first.

Frank adored his wife.

As for Mark, he probably wasn't capable of love. Still, deep down he knew that on the remote chance it ever did happen to him, he'd be full-on committed like this man. If he fell, he'd fall hard.

Cassie turned when they reached the weathered steps leading up to her bungalow. Her hand landed on his tensing bicep. "Thank you for helping me," she said slowly.

His gaze jumped to her soft face then swerved to the bleak sky. "You're welcome. Good night," he muttered and strode away without waiting for a response.

Deep down he knew he wanted more than words from her. He wanted what he couldn't have. Cassie, her beautiful body wrapped around him as he moved inside her.

6

CASSIE SIPPED HER tea in the makeshift nurses station the next evening and tapped in her email password on one of the newly erected field hospital's shared computers. As it was one of the few devices on the island that was hardwired for internet after the hurricane knocked out Wi-Fi, it'd been in demand all day. Near the end of her shift, to her surprise, she'd found it unoccupied and decided to check in with her family.

Immediately, fifteen emails from her mother caught her eye. The subject line of the first was a simple "Hi!" but things had escalated to "Are You Dead?" by the last. Didn't her mother understand how difficult communications were? She had taken care to go over it.

Guilt settled hard and heavy in her gut. She'd known her leaving would take a large toll on her mother, especially as it'd remind her of losing Jeff. Still, this was important. For the first time in her life, Cassie hadn't let herself be swayed or stopped by her mother's anxiety.

She clicked on the last message and dropped her chin to her palms, elbows propped up on the desk.

Cassie,
I haven't slept in a week. Why haven't you responded
to my emails? Are you safe? Eating? Getting enough
rest? Staying indoors? I've been watching the news
and the pictures are terrifying. Can you come home
now? I don't think I can last much longer.
Love,
Mom

Cassie rubbed her throbbing temples then quickly
typed:

Mom,
I have to keep this short because other people need
to use the computer. But, good news! I'm alive. Even
better, I'm safe. I'm sorry that you're so worried and I
don't want you to get so sick that you have to go back
to the hospital, okay? Please get some sleep and take
care of yourself. I'll be home really soon. Just another
week until I can beat you at Monopoly like always. Better practice with Dad since I'll be gunning for you ☺.
I miss you and can't wait to go home!
Love,
Cassie

After logging out, she evacuated the seat for another eager internet surfer and headed for the sink to
rinse out her cup.

Can't wait to go home, she'd written. She stared at
her reflection.

Liar.

She didn't miss home. In fact, being here was a relief
from her mother's ever-present, oppressive fear. Was

it crazy to feel more relaxed in the middle of a disaster than surrounded by her mother's frenetic energy?

Probably. Even more insane were her nonstop thoughts of Mark.

She dried her cup and placed it on a shelf before turning back again to pump soap into her palm.

Yesterday, he'd been a man of action. Decisive. Certain. If not for his take-charge attitude that'd quieted a hysterical Jacque and steadied Cassie, they might not have saved Eloise. Yet he'd looked as shaken as she had once the rescue was over, showing a vulnerability that made him more human. More like the man who'd made love to her so passionately.

Her body heated at the memory, a match for the warm water running over her sudsy hands. She rubbed her fingers together methodically, washing each knuckle, digit and nail. Diligence was priceless in her profession.

If only she took as much care in her personal life.

She shouldn't be thinking about Mark.

Grabbing a couple of paper towels from the folded stack, she dried off, stepped on the garbage pail's opener and tossed them inside.

She'd come on this mission to honor Jeff and his legacy. Not for romance. End of story.

At least when it came to her and Mark.

She shook off her thoughts and put on one of those smiles that wasn't really a smile at all as she headed out to treat her last patient. Whirring ventilators sucked acrid air out of the large domed space. To the right, entrances opened to an OR, a radiology unit, a maternity ward and an ICU where she'd looked in on Eloise earlier this afternoon and noticed Mark departing.

What a relief to see the woman recovering from open-heart surgery.

After passing several beds, she reached her patient, PO1 Ian McClaughlin, one of the rescue swimmers who'd flown to St. Thomas with her and Mark's crew.

"Hello, Ian. Time for a dressing change."

The sandy-haired rescue swimmer opened his eyes, his expression clear now that the heavier pain meds had worn off. Light freckles stood out against his pale skin. A large bandage covered a six-inch gash on his cheek that'd taken almost a hundred stitches to close, according to the chart.

"Cassie, right?"

"Right. How are you feeling?" She glanced at him sideways as she unscrewed the top off the silver sulfadiazine then grabbed a pair of gloves from a nearby box.

"I can handle it." His lips twisted in a wan smile and he held out his hands.

After checking his facial wound for infection, she carefully lifted the foam from each finger. She studied the abrasion burns he'd received when a severed, frayed hoist cable ripped through his gloves before slashing his face.

"You're brave." Holding a basin beneath his hands, she washed the raw, blistered skin.

"Just doing my job." His matter-of-fact tone caught her off guard. Didn't he bear any resentment? During the morning report out, Cassie had learned that the crew he'd worked with the night before—which flew opposite shifts to Mark's—had had to return to base without him when they couldn't repair the equipment before running out of fuel.

"Were you upset when the helicopter left you?" Using a sterile cloth, she patted his fingers dry.

Ian stared up at the ceiling and shook his head. "They had to follow procedures or put the entire crew and the survivors we'd just rescued at risk. I wouldn't want that. No swimmer would."

Cassie imagined Jeff and knew, as sure as she knew anything, that he would have felt the same way. Was it possible that safeguarding others played a bigger role in Jeff's tragedy than the actions of a heartless pilot?

"But weren't you worried?" she persisted, needing answers, hoping she didn't push the injured swimmer too far.

"I knew they'd be back." His jagged voice rose.

She smoothed on the ointment, one part of her brain hyper-focused on her job, the other part adrift with Jeff. "How did you know?"

"We're brothers," he said proudly. "A family. We always have each other's back, don't abandon each other."

"But what if they didn't find you in time?"

They left Jeff at sea. Her hands trembled as she wrapped fresh dressings around Ian's fingers.

But they had come back for him...too late.

Could the crew—could Mark—have viewed Jeff this way...a brother lost at sea? If so, Raeanne's comments about Mark being broken up, unable to fly, made sense.

"If they didn't rescue me, I'd have ridden a wave to the end, a true brother of the fin, right?" He gave her a cocky grin before growing serious again. "We don't do this job for glory. You know our motto, right?"

She nodded, her throat swelling. "So others may

live." Jeff's Facebook wall, plastered with the saying, flashed in her mind's eye.

"Every day that I jump in the water, I accept that I might not come out. What's important is giving my all and saving others. As long as I do that, I'll be proud, right up to the end…"

Suddenly, it was too much. "Excuse me," she choked out then dashed up the aisle, fighting back her tears.

After a report out, she bolted outside, gusty air cool on her burning cheeks. The worst images she had imagined of Jeff alone in a furious ocean howled inside her.

Then, like the eye of a storm, her shaking muscles stilled and a new picture rose, slightly out of focus. Jeff, no longer scared but calm.

Hurrying toward her housing unit, she told herself to get her head together. Make sense of the kaleidoscope images that shifted and spun, making her dizzy.

A group of servicemen passed her, their olive green flight suits reminding her of Jeff, making her shoulders hunch. She stopped short outside her door.

She'd thought she wanted to be alone, but now she realized what she really wanted, needed, was answers. Mark knew the truth of what had happened that day, and she deserved to know, damn it.

She stopped one of the men, asked for directions and headed to their dorms. As she climbed the steps to the bungalows' shared porch, Mark emerged from one of the rooms.

"Mark!" she yelled. In an instant, he reached her side.

"Are you okay?" The timbre of his voice, low and gentle, loosened the hard knot in her chest. How much did she wish he could be a good guy?

"No." They stared at each other. She wanted to look away, but couldn't. All she could see were his big eyes, darkening to amber, the backs of his strong hands, the way his torso shifted under his flight suit.

"What happened?" Concern turned his question into staccato beats. They nearly undid her.

"A long day. Look. I want to talk to—" Suddenly, she swayed on her feet and he caught her firmly around the waist.

She opened her mouth to protest but was overwhelmed by the prickling awareness of his fingers on the bare skin under the loose hem of her shirt.

"Dylan," Mark called to an approaching crew member she recognized from their flight. "Inform the guys I'll be there shortly. Go ahead and start the equipment checks."

Dylan studied them both before nodding and striding away.

Mark ushered her inside his neat room. She perched on the end of the bed and her body heated at the memory of the time she'd been in his Clearwater hotel room.

He handed her a couple of energy bars and a bottled water. "Eat this. You can rest here as long as you want. I don't want you wandering around and getting lost again," he said, a teasing note entering his voice. "If you need anything else just let me know," he offered, though he was already turning to leave.

She placed the items on the nightstand. "There is. Tell me about the day Jeff disappeared."

At her quiet words, he froze in the doorway. The muscles in his jaw visibly clenched; pain and guilt blurred his breathtaking profile.

Seconds scraped by in painful silence.

"You've read everything," he said, staring outside. His shoulders rose and he looked like he was braced for a blow. Had no plans of ducking it.

"I want to hear what happened to you."

"Me? Nothing happened to me," he exclaimed, yet his tortured expression told another, harsher story. He kicked the door shut with the back of his heel and strode to the bed. "Jeff is the one who matters."

Not just him came the unbidden thought, catching her off guard. Mark mattered, too, she realized. He mattered to her.

"If you cared about Jeff, then you'll tell me. Please." Something she couldn't quite identify broke over her like a vast wave.

He swallowed hard and then let out a long, slow, shuddering breath. The mattress dipped as he sat beside her and his thumbs gently brushed the dampness from her cheeks. When her lids lifted, she met his large eyes, so close to hers. She wouldn't cry again, not when Mark deserved her clear-eyed and ready to hear him out.

"It was a routine mission."

Her stomach lurched. "Not all of it."

He bowed his rigid face. "Jeff put the last survivor in the basket."

"He must have been—" She swallowed hard and tried again. "He must have been happy about that."

Mark shot her a surprised look. "Yeah. He was. He did that lasso thing…"

The image of her exuberant, larger-than-life brother hit like a punch. She waited until the humming in her mind leached away to nothing, and then said, "That was his yippee-ki-yay signal."

Mark raked a shaking hand through his hair, making the ends stand up at odd angles. "He loved all the *Die Hard* movies."

"I think he made me watch them a hundred times. His favorite was *Live Free or Die Hard*." She stared at the dark curtains covering Mark's window, picturing the movie, wishing she could see it with Jeff one more time.

"He always picked one of them when it was his turn for movie night." One side of Mark's mouth curved up then fell. "Man, we were sick of them."

Outside, she could hear the acoustics of early evening in the resort's staging area, the whine of distant engines, a car door slamming, a dog barking at some unseen outrage. Life in its messy, vital entirety. It matched her own tangled emotions—humor and despair, loss and discovery. "After he made the lasso signal, what happened?"

"We were thirty-five feet over the water. I was sitting right seat, which meant I was at the flight controls. The flight mechanic lowered the rescue hook for Jeff." Mark rubbed his jaw and the circles beneath his eyes were ash colored. "But the cable got wrapped around the tail wheel. When Larry pulled it back and inspected it, he didn't find any visible kinks or degradation. Basically, it was fine, but we always check it three times."

"And did you…?" Her words failed, her breath faltering.

Mark reached out his hands slowly, enfolding hers and holding them until she could speak again.

"Did you make sure?" The warmth of his strong hands made her feel secure. Anchored.

"We had less than five minutes to retrieve him before we hit BINGO." He swallowed hard. "That's the critical point on deciding whether to stay or go because of our fuel level. I gave the order to lower it to Jeff without the third check." His voice was slightly slurred, its edges frayed with pain.

"And it snapped," she whispered, recalling the notation "hoist cable parted" as the cause of the accident. There was a painful crushing sensation in the center of her chest, as if someone were trying to flatten her.

He didn't speak, but dipped his head so that it came to rest against hers. They sat there in the dark room, breathing in the balmy air, listening to the muffled sound of service personnel talking as they passed by. "I didn't get Jeff aboard." His voice, when it emerged, was gruff...broken.

"The cable didn't get Jeff aboard," she corrected. Understanding swelled. Mark wasn't a monster. He wouldn't have left Jeff if he'd had another choice. It was easy to see how much this ripped him apart.

His eyes blazed at her suddenly. "I was responsible for the hoist cable's entire evolution. The crew. Every single thing on that aircraft. Everything that happened on the mission. Don't you get it?" He yanked his hands away and balled them on jittering knees.

"I don't blame you, Mark. Not anymore."

He bolted to his feet, his body tense and movements jerky. "You *should* blame me," he ground out and paced to the window. "It's my fault."

Cassie clasped her hands in front of her. "I don't agree."

"You don't know." He stopped at the bed and dropped to his knees. He cupped her face with an aching tenderness and all of her nerves concentrated there, alive to every movement of his skin on hers. "I'm sorry, Cassie. If I could trade places with Jeff, I would."

"Jeff wouldn't want that," she said automatically, then realized, with a start, how true those words were. Jeff always put others first. He wouldn't have switched places with Mark for anything.

He rubbed his eyes with the heels of his hands, suddenly looking very tired. "I failed him. You. Your family."

"You tried to save him. You had no choice but to leave after the cable snapped, especially since you were running low on fuel."

"I should have checked it a third time. It was still my call. My mission."

"Would checking it again have kept it from snapping?"

He shook his head but seemed about to argue.

"I'm glad Jeff was with you—" she began, and her voice cracked as she recalled how highly he'd spoken of his crew members, the brotherhood Ian reminded her about. "Though it must have been so hard for you to leave him—"

Mark's mouth opened and pain made a mask of his face, warping each feature. Then he lowered his head and closed his eyes.

All this time she'd focused solely on how hard it was for her, but hearing Mark, seeing his suffering, confirmed what she'd suspected after talking to Ian. Jeff had been Mark's brother, too, and losing him had destroyed Mark as much as it had her.

She'd been harboring so much anger at Mark—even before they'd met—never realizing he might be the one person who felt the same kind of grief she did.

Her chest ached for the man before her and what he'd gone through that day. Regret stung. She'd accused him of leaving Jeff, when it must have ripped him up to make that impossible call to fly away.

She pulled him to his feet and fitted her body to his, every nerve ending screaming to life as her curves pressed against his rigid body.

She didn't want to hurt anymore.

MARK'S MOUTH WAS the consistency of powder. His heart pounded so hard he could barely suck in air. Paralyzed by his own longing, his gaze dropped to Cassie's full mouth and his crotch tightened. It was a painful reminder of how much he wanted her—in this moment, and every moment since they'd met. For the past couple of nights, he'd gone to sleep craving her. Woken each morning, rock hard, his body slick and aching with need.

And now here she was in his room, tempting him. He shouldn't touch her, but being this close, talking to her, had torn away his last damn defense.

Heat sizzled in her blue eyes and the small space between her front teeth appeared in an alluring smile. And then, lust took over, hitting him hot and hard, his fierce attraction needy, edgy and demanding. It was too much to resist kissing her. He dragged her closer still, wrapping her in his arms.

She was sexy. So damn sexy.

Too lost in the moment to speak, he slid his fingers down along her jawline and she shivered against him, leaning her cheek into his touch. When her hands smoothed over the shorn hair at his nape, his ears rang. His heart thrummed. Everything inside him twisted with the urge to touch her. To feel her skin beneath his palms, under his mouth.

Mark slipped his hand from her chin to cradle her head. His fingers tunneled through her silky hair and her head tipped back, a soft cry escaping her. Her breath was warm against his face as he hovered his lips above hers.

"Please," she whimpered.

Blood pounded wildly in his veins. A magnetic pull seemed to be taking over the small distance between their mouths. An energy he couldn't resist. Especially when her tongue darted out to lick her lips, an incredibly hot move that could bring a grown man crashing to his knees. As it was, he had to snake an arm around her waist to hold them both up as she melted against him. He inclined his head and she closed her eyes as their mouths crashed together.

He inhaled her breath, its traces of something cinnamon and berry, the warm, wet taste of her. God, he wanted this. Wanted her.

Angling his head, he slid his tongue along the seam of her mouth. His lips moved over hers until she opened her mouth. Their tongues slid over each other, stroking and rubbing, taking. Giving. The sensation was intoxicating. Tiny explosions burst inside him. He couldn't think, couldn't focus.

He backed her against the bed and they dropped to its plush comforter, her hands smoothing over his shoulders and stroking his back. When her mouth left his to trail along his jaw, he explored, too, sucking on her earlobe until her breath grew ragged.

Her back arched and her knees rose to grip his hips. His pulse raced as she rubbed against his bulging crotch, only his thin flight suit and her scrubs separating them.

The memory of the night they met returned, making his cock strain and jerk. How wet she'd been. Hot. Soft. He groaned, wanting to bury himself in her again.

"Mark," she whispered in his ear and her fingers skimmed down his lower back, her hands squeezing his butt before coming around to stroke his rigid length. He shuddered against her, her touch setting him on fire.

"So hot," he murmured and then his mouth captured hers again as he gripped her waist, grinding against her. He kissed her harder now, his lungs burning as his breath came in fits and starts. He traced the nipples straining beneath her shirt, rolling them between his fingers. Her breath caught against his lips when he cupped her breasts fully and he reveled in her reaction. Power, intense and gratifying, surged through him.

"Yes," she cried, meeting his gaze head-on. He could see the desire glowing in her eyes as the same response took his body by storm.

His hands trembled as he unsnapped her top and slid the material off her shoulders. His heart thumped erratically at the sight of her straining nipples against the plain white fabric of her bra. Even in the most practical undergarments, she turned him on like no other. He wanted to lose himself in her.

"Beautiful," he rasped and ran a finger beneath the bottom edge as their mouths met.

Pushing down the fabric, he bared her breasts and pulled back to admire them. Light gold, with a cute tan line across the top, her breasts were full, the tips a deep rose, beaded and begging. A small gold locket nestled between them, and he wanted to take its place.

"Perfection."

She whimpered as he traced her areolas with his tongue then pulled at each, her body straining beneath him at the shared, decadent pleasure. He lifted each globe, suckling them harder as need burned through his body; he was practically shaking with it.

She gripped his hips, pulling him closer still. When he stroked the creamy flesh of her abdomen, his hands traveling lower, then lower still, her head thrashed on the pillow and a low moan escaped her.

His own breath quickened. He drew down her panties more roughly than he intended but Cassie didn't seem to mind. Her fingers kneaded into his shoulders. Dug in hard enough to sting. He nudged her legs apart and she watched him, her gaze slightly unfocused, lips parted, hair tangling around her face, looking wanton.

Something softened inside him at the way she gave herself to him, so totally uninhibited and unselfconscious. She was a woman who had lost much, yet she'd opened up to the very man who'd caused her pain. And how the hell had he ended up thinking this now when he lay between her thighs and the blood pounded in his ears louder than the surf hit the shore outside?

But as her silvery eyes looked up at him, so giving and warm, he knew he would do everything in his power to make sure her trust wasn't misplaced. Nobody hurt Cassie on his watch. Not even Mark.

Then her thighs wrapped around his waist the way they had on the beach the night they'd met, and all else was lost in a tide of pure sensation.

Only the need to imprint himself on her memory remained.

He reached between their bodies to caress the tender damp heat of her. She whimpered. Cried out. Thick lashes fanned atop her flushed cheeks. He circled her swollen clit again and again, teasing her so that she strained against him with arched hips. Bucking against his hand.

"Open your eyes," he whispered raggedly. Won the attention of her passion-clouded gaze.

He increased the pressure of his finger then slid it inside, adding another. Her silken flesh clamped around him, convulsing. Their eyes locked in a blazing hot instant. Barely keeping himself in check, he plunged deeper, faster. He watched her features sharpen and her mouth fall open as she panted, moving with the rhythm of his hand. Continuing to flick her clit with his slick thumb, he thrust his fingers ever deeper, stroking her inner walls.

A thick throb of desire pulsed in his gut. He wanted to erase her pain, replace it with earth-shattering pleasure. The fierceness of that need gripped him with undeniable force.

Soon her gasps matched his tempo of his thrusts and he intensified his movements, going faster, harder, until at last she cried out, the primal sound shattering the last of his control, making his pulse skyrocket. He had to be inside her. Now. Needed to end this torment with the explosive release only they could give each other.

Then, something metallic caught his eye.

The locket around her neck had opened.

Inside was Jeff's grinning face, sharp canines appearing in a familiar smile.

Holy shit.

What was he doing here with Jeff's sister? As if he had any right to be with her, to lose himself completely in Cassie.

He scrambled off the bed and turned away, his chest rising and falling as he grappled with the emotions threatening to drag him under.

"Mark?" A soft hand fell on his shoulder and he stiffened.

"I can't do this."

She ducked in front of him and tried catching his eye. "I don't blame you. I—I forgive you."

He jerked away and headed to the door. Opening it, he paused in the entrance and turned, the vise around his chest tightening at her anguished expression.

"That makes one of us."

And with that, he headed outside like he damn well should have thirty minutes earlier.

Crap. What the hell had he done?

A strong island breeze ruffled his hair and swung his flight bag like a limp sail as he trudged on the path to the landing strip's shuttle. He couldn't think while kissing Cassie. For a moment, she'd made the familiar hurt he'd carried since Jeff's death recede and it'd felt too good to stop.

And before that, when she'd asked him about the day Jeff had disappeared, he'd been able to open up, despite the pain, recounting details he'd locked away.

Was it as much his fault as he'd assumed?

Downed branches snapped under his boots as he marched on.

No. He wouldn't give himself such an easy out. That was weakness and he was man enough to admit his wrongs.

Wouldn't let go of that hurt.

Didn't deserve to.

Jeff couldn't get the life back Mark had cost him. And Mark sure as hell didn't deserve to have a life now, either. Not one full of things Jeff would never enjoy. Definitely not one that included Jeff's sister.

Mark wouldn't dishonor his friend by being with her, or risk his crew's safety by letting thoughts of her distract him.

Tomorrow, he'd request a switch to night flights. With his schedule flipped, he'd be less likely to see her again during this mission.

Cassie forgiving him was crazy. She didn't understand what she said. Their attraction must be blinding her from the truth. With some time apart, she'd remember every reason she should hate him.

The thought cut him through and he stopped on the trail. He studied a tall bush, stripped bare of its blooms, as it bent back and forth with the ever-present wind.

His life was just like that. Following whatever direction fate pointed him in. Why should he get to choose his destiny when Jeff couldn't?

He'd joined the Coast Guard to be a hero but he'd fallen. Rising again required hard work, discipline, focus and sacrifice.

At the top of his sacrifice list: Cassie.

Why, for a moment, had he thought it okay to be with her?

Cassie was supposed to be just a memory. An incredible one-night stand that had left him wanting more. But she'd delved deeper, become embedded, and he didn't know how to dig her out, so he'd avoid her instead.

He damn well didn't deserve her.

7

"THANK YOU, CAPTAIN VOGT. This means a lot to me."

Cassie shook the TACON mission commander's hand and strode from his office the following afternoon, the synapses in her brain firing full throttle.

She'd done it. Her nursing shoes squelched on the tiled floor as she stepped briskly to the commandeered resort office's supply room. Polish and glass cleaner. Fresh paint. Despite the recent devastation, the smell of renewal surrounded her—life marching on. Maybe this was her chance to do the same.

With Marjorie Little's recommendation, and her own list of credentials that included being a qualified emergency medical technician with flight nurse training, she'd gained permission to stand in for Mark's injured medic tomorrow while they waited for a replacement.

She passed a bank of windows and lifted her hair off her neck, hoping to catch the breeze that bent the large hibiscus bushes lining the circular drive out front. All those years spent driving to Boise for post-RN training were finally being put to use. She'd never thought she'd use them, and had been almost surprised by the long list when she'd detailed her extra certifications to both Nurse Little and the commander. She'd achieved a lot during her seven years after nursing school. Then again, how else to while away the time in a small town? It wasn't like hot pilots dropped out of the Idaho skies.

A couple of men wearing formal navy uniforms nodded politely to her as they passed. What would Mark look like in his dress blues? So far she'd only glimpsed him in his olive flight suit, but his mouth-watering, muscular body did that uniform all kinds of good.

Desire rose, warm and pulsing between her thighs, and she forced her mind off how incredibly aroused and sexually frustrated he'd made her the day before. If not for his rejection, she would have slept with him. The man she'd once blamed for her brother's death.

Could she have lived with that?

Yes, came the immediate answer as she rounded a corner, pulled open a glass-paned door and strode to an empty counter. She dinged the bell and waited, leaning against the rounded edge, sliding one aching toe out of her shoe then the other.

She admired Mark. He'd done everything he could to save her brother.

Had he put the brakes on sex out of guilt? Denied them pleasure as a form of penance?

If so, she needed to get through to him. Make him see that he couldn't control everything, including Jeff's fate.

A young woman appeared wearing a light blue shirt tucked into navy pants. Trops, she'd heard this less formal uniform called. She handed the clerk the slip

Captain Vogt had given her and returned the woman's smile. Alone again, she arched her back and straightened her shoulder slump. Her break ended soon and she needed to reboot for the second half of her shift... and what promised to be a busy night this evening as the Red Cross put on a large-scale supply giveaway to avoid stockpiling in the already crowded hospital unit. And, of course, that would be followed by an action-packed day tomorrow.

Flying with Mark would help her get to know the brooding pilot better. Maybe even pursue a relationship with him—if only temporarily. Based on his reaction yesterday, however, she knew it'd be difficult convincing him.

Not that taking the easy path was her style anymore...

She thrived on this relief mission's challenges and a part of her wanted to live life to the fullest the way Jeff had advised. Flying with his old crew would give her a closer perspective on her brother's world and the risks he'd taken.

And maybe, finally, she'd gain the closure she needed to feel at peace again when she returned to her old life. Funny how small that life looked from this distance.

Five minutes later, Cassie hurried from the supply area, a flight suit draped across her arm.

"What are you doing?"

She pulled up short at the familiar, commanding voice and turned.

In a gray muscle shirt and black gym shorts, Mark was a ripped, lean machine. She couldn't help admiring his large deltoids and the tantalizing outline of his six-pack abs through the thin fabric. Defined thigh muscles shifted and bulged as he strode forward, closing the distance between them.

He jerked to a stop and crossed his arms, giving her an eyeful of corded biceps. When she stared into his piercing gold eyes, her body hummed with a sexual rush.

Another man cleared his throat and she spared a quick glance at Mark's companion from the other night. Dylan.

"I'll wait outside." The other large, muscle-bound man shot Mark a considering look before heading down the hallway.

She extended the arm holding the flight suit. "I'm filling in for your injured flight medic, John, until a new AST3 arrives. I treated him this morning and heard you needed a replacement."

"No." Mark's nostrils flared and a muscle jumped in his square jaw, his expression thunderous.

"Captain Vogt just approved it. He's calling your command boss now." Despite the angry sparks shooting from his eyes, she stepped forward. Guilt made her want to take back her request given how awful Mark felt about Jeff's death. It was asking a lot from him to fly with her. Yet she had to persevere and take this final step into Jeff's—and Mark's—world to gain the understanding she needed to put the loss behind her. "I want to fly with Jeff's crew."

Mark opened his mouth then shut it when a couple of service personnel passed by, their conversation fading as they shot each other speculative glances.

"Follow me," he ordered then turned sharply on his

heel and tramped down the hall to a large walk-in storage area.

When he reached around to shut the door behind her, her heart rate tripled at his nearness.

"I'm not letting you fly on any missions," he bit out, his lion's gaze raking over her.

"It's not your choice to make." She crossed her arms and widened her stance. Sympathy for Mark fired through her, but maybe if she could find the right words, explain to him why this was important, he'd understand…

He arched a brow, his expression so arrogant she didn't know if she wanted to smack him or kiss him. "It's my aircraft."

"It's Captain Vogt's call." She edged closer until they stood toe to toe. The spicy, masculine scent of him rose around them and she breathed deep.

His eyes traveled slowly from her mouth to her feet then back up again, looking her over with such intensity that Cassie's toes curled. "It's not safe," he insisted, though a note of hoarseness had entered his voice.

"I'm not worried about that."

"You should be," he burst out. "Besides, my rescue swimmers are already Level 1 EMTs. I've seen you do CPR but I need someone with more specific skills."

"In addition to being a registered nurse," she spouted quickly, hoping to impress him, "I'm also flight nurse registered, an intravenous certified specialist, an advanced burn life support provider, cardiac-vascular nursing certified and wound care certified." She angled her chin and met his eye.

Mark raised an eyebrow. "And you did all this in Horseshoe Bend, Idaho?"

Hearing her hometown come out of his mouth took her aback until she remembered. He would know it because of Jeff. "It's not the back of beyond," she defended, though it felt like it at times…

Had the claustrophobia she'd felt in the small town driven her to commute to Boise and continue her professional development? Working for her father and living at home left her restless and craving a purpose. Those classes and credentials helped, even though she'd never thought she'd use them until now.

He placed a hand on the door behind her head and leaned in, eyes glittering. "But you don't have real-life emergency flight experience."

She ducked under his arm and strode farther into the walk-in closet. "So give it to me. I'll prove you wrong."

He whirled and closed the distance between them again, his jaw clenched. "I'm not taking that chance. You're my responsibility and I want you here, where you're safe."

Her sharp intake of breath reverberated in the stillness. How many times had she heard those words from her oppressive mother growing up? Believed them?

Jeff the brave.

Cassie the meek.

She used to think she wasn't like Jeff. Couldn't grab the world and ride its orbit as it spun. But now…now she wondered if her mother's worries stemmed from nearly losing Cassie thanks to her premature birth. Not a weakness in Cassie, exactly.

As for Mark, his lack of faith stung, too. He needed to see her bolder side. She didn't want to wear the yoke of others' fears any longer and would prove just how daring she could be.

Setting the flight suit aside on a shelf, she placed her hand on his hard abdomen, feeling the muscular ridges contract beneath her fingers. "I understand you're worried after what happened to Jeff—"

"Anything can happen out there," he cut her off. "I'm not putting you at risk." Air separated his words, as if he struggled to breathe.

With him this close, her lungs weren't working well, either. "I trust you," she whispered and stood on tiptoe to wrap her arms around his neck.

He caught her wrists in one hand. "Stop it, Cassie," he demanded, though his eyes were liquid want, heavy with longing. The sexual tension between them grew electric, crackling with its own magnetic pull. "Why is this so important to you?"

"Because I want to feel close to Jeff. I need to put myself back together by honoring his life," she cried, yanking loose. "Flying with you, performing his missions, will give me that chance."

Mark ran the back of his knuckles down the side of her cheek, and she ached at the pain in his eyes.

"I'm doing the same thing," he admitted, sinking his eyes deeply into hers. "Every successful mission I fly here, every rescue I make, is helping me accept what happened. I—I grounded myself after we lost Jeff. I was in a bad place."

He dropped his hand and averted his gaze before continuing. "I was out of the cockpit for six months, talking to doctors, talking to therapists, talking, talking, talking until they believed I could fly again…only once this disaster mission came up, and memories of Jeff hit me hard, I stopped being convinced. I replay that hoist accident every single day. What if I'd moved left versus right? What if I'd instructed the flight mechanic to watch for rogue waves? What if I'd been five feet lower? What if? What if?"

"And then I showed up," she murmured, fully understanding now just how hard it must have been for him to see her at this all-important moment, when he needed to prove to himself, once and for all, that he had moved past Jeff's loss. "I get it."

Mark rubbed his eyes, hard. "Our night on the beach was perfect. Exactly what I needed to stop the replay button."

A short laugh escaped her. "That's how I felt. I might not have made it onto the helicopter if not for you. Now I'm ready for the next step."

"You're still going tomorrow." His eyes swerved to hers, sharp and intent.

She jerked back, stung. "I thought you understood."

"I thought *you* understood," he insisted, his voice strained, as if he'd been sucker punched. "I can't focus with you on board. Why are you pushing me into a position that's going to cloud my judgment in the air?"

"Because I can't have closure unless I go."

"So your mind's made up." At her nod, he turned and her chest constricted at the pained, grim expression on his face. How she wished this could be different. That they were on the same side, holding each other as they had on the beach.

"Mark, please. Understand—" she began, faltering, trying to find the words to convince him, panicked that she hadn't. When Mark reached the door, he spoke with his face averted, his shoulders high and tense.

"No, Cassie. I don't," he snapped, his tone bitter.

"As the commander of Jayhawk copter 6039, I have the final say. You will not fly on my aircraft. Period."

The door clicked shut behind him and her last glimpse of Mark's tormented expression curled her insides. She dropped her head into her hands and shook, struggling to regain the confidence that'd been slowly building since she'd arrived on Saint Thomas.

Mark, of all people, should understand how important flying in Jeff's aircraft would be to her. After everything they'd been through, how could he care so little about what she needed?

She stood there for a moment then brushed off her pants and jerked open the door, head high.

No matter what, she'd ride on their next mission.

FORTY MINUTES LATER, Mark dropped to a squat on the tarmac, winded. The pavement was a warm pulse beneath his palms as he kicked his feet back again, executed two more push-ups, brought his feet back to his hands and leaped for the sky, the last move in this latest eight-count burpee. Gripping the back end of a door-less club car, a man-size military vehicle issued on these missions, he rolled it fifty yards across the resort's empty back parking lot toward Dylan. The slow, sweet pull of his muscles felt good after spending so much time cramped in a cockpit. They'd been relieved early today and he'd been looking forward to this hard-driving workout…until he'd spotted Cassie with a flight suit.

"That all you got?" jeered the cocky swimmer. He stopped the automobile's roll, plunged to the ground, fired off one-armed push-ups before jumping as high as the car roof. With his cropped curls lying flat against his head, Dylan reminded Mark of one of those Roman soldiers he'd watched in movies or played in video games. His Herculean proportions only furthered the effect.

"Didn't want to embarrass you," Mark called, his lungs afire. While Dylan worked through his set, Mark struggled to catch his breath. He dragged the hurricane-scrubbed fresh air into his lungs, the temperature almost ten degrees cooler than normal now that a low-pressure system had pulled the storm a bit farther north where it squatted over the Atlantic. It moved eastward at fifteen nautical miles per hour, the slow pace building its intensity.

His insides brewed along with it.

Why was Cassie so intent on joining his crew? He'd explained more to her than he'd even fully explained to himself, yet she acted as though none of that mattered, as if he didn't matter.

"Incoming." With a grunt, Dylan shoved the club car back at Mark. "How many more you got in you?"

"More than you," Mark shot back and halted the vehicle. Swimmers. Always so damn competitive. Though he needed to be pushed today...even more than he'd thought when he'd sought out Dylan earlier.

Sweat dripped in his eyes as he dropped to the ground again. Getting through to Cassie looked less difficult than it had. He needed to change her mind.

His breath rasped in his throat as he added more push-ups to his set. He shoved the car back at Dylan, who, annoyingly, had been doing crunches during his downtime. Did these rescue athletes ever quit?

Mark held his aching sides and bent at the waist. His late-afternoon shadow angled to his left and ran up the bark of a ragged palm tree. The only sounds were the birdsong, the gentle murmur of the breeze through the trees and the distant lapping of low tide.

An exclamation of air escaped through his gritted teeth. Maybe all she wanted from him was sex.

A lizard skittered in front of him then clambered across a slanted tree trunk ahead of the returning club car.

He needed this exercise more than ever, his pent-up sexual energy at an all-time high.

It shouldn't bug him if Cassie saw him only in terms of sex. What man didn't want to be objectified? But it didn't sit right, damn it. She'd slipped past his defenses and now he couldn't shake her loose.

"That was a twelve-count," Dylan catcalled, his voice as fresh as when they'd started.

"Amateur hour." Mark ignored his protesting muscles and whipped himself through an extra cycle. "Top that."

The club car kicked up a pebble when he thrust it away again, his arms shaking.

"I'm just getting started." Dylan's lip curled.

Mark grabbed his water bottle from his calf holder, gulped down a mouthful then doused his burning head for good measure. When he tossed the empty container at a receptacle, a couple of gulls squawked and flapped before settling to roost atop stone pavers.

He'd been slowly rebuilding his tattered confidence with each successful mission the past few days. Now Cassie threatened to tear it down for good by flying with him. How could he focus when a part of him would worry about keeping her safe? When another part of him would relive the last time he'd flown into danger carrying a Rowe.

He had to stop Cassie, but how?

"Sixteen!" Dylan leaned on the club car's hood, his chest barely rising or falling. Was he even human?

"I'm going to stop you there before you hurt yourself, kid. Let's run."

"Asshole." They pushed the vehicle back into its spot for other workout teams and headed to the beach. At the trailhead, they stopped to stretch. He pulled his heel to his back and his mind drifted again to Cassie.

Despite his tough words, he couldn't actually refuse her assignment on his aircraft. He could call his command boss and ask him to intervene with Captain Vogt, but Mark would need a logical reason for the request.

He didn't question her abilities, just her frame of mind. Cassie was more than qualified to be a flight medic, her surprising list of advanced certifications impressive. What plausible excuse could he give? Not the truth. If he revealed that flying with Jeff's sister rattled his nerves, his superiors would question whether Mark could fly at all…if he'd truly conquered his demons.

And he had. Or he'd thought he had, until Cassie.

"Hey. You in there?" He looked up from his stretch and Dylan tossed him a couple more water bottles.

"Didn't hear you." He slipped the containers into his running belt before reaching for his toes.

Dylan's mouth twisted in a smile. "Losing your hearing already? Shit. Getting old sucks."

He socked Dylan in the shoulder. "Watch your mouth, son. Thirty-one isn't old. Want me to prove it?"

Dylan threw his hands in the air and backed up a step, laughing. He pulled on a neon yellow headband bright enough to make Mark squint. "I'll take your word for it. Or…you could try keeping up."

With that, Dylan sprinted down the path and disappeared around a bend.

"You son of a—" Mark darted after the rescue swimmer, his legs pumping, feet churning up the loose dirt and leaves. Vegetation caught at his shins, ripping at his skin, but his adrenaline rushed too hard to let him feel it. Instead, he breathed in the salted air, fragranced with the lightest trace of flowers, a sign the island had begun to heal.

As for himself…not so much it seemed.

He caught up to Dylan on the beach and the sun splashed directly in his face, momentarily blinding him.

"Hey, glad you could keep up after all." Dylan's arms swung as he ran across the sand. Five yards down, the clear, aquamarine ocean swirled against the white shore.

"Try keeping up with this." Mark pushed ahead, setting a blistering pace. His sneakers plunged in and out of the powdery surface, the resistance welcome. He listened to the pounding of his own heart, the familiar rasp of his breath, and the tense knot inside his gut began to uncoil.

The sun bobbed over the horizon. Storm clouds lingered to the north. They'd be flying in that direction tomorrow he'd been told, when his request to change shifts had been refused.

Something cold stole around his heart when he imagined Cassie aboard, a chill in spite of the tropical heat and his own rising temperature.

"So why the hermit act lately?" Dylan huffed beside him.

"What?" He whipped off his damp shirt and stuffed the collar in the elastic band of his shorts.

Dylan grabbed one of his water bottles and squirted the liquid in his mouth. "You haven't been around much. The guys are starting to think you're seeing someone else."

"Can you blame me? You're too young, too slow and your taste in workout gear sucks. Our relationship was going nowhere."

"Seriously, dude. What's up?" Dylan slipped his container back into the holder and kept pace.

"Nada," he said, trying to shut the conversation down, wherever it was going. The whoosh of the sea grew louder as the tide crept higher on the deserted, debris-littered beach. His feet crunched over broken shells and dried seaweed, his eyes staring straight ahead at the downed trees on the formerly lush mountainside.

"We all knew coming on our first, large-scale disaster response mission without Jeff was going to be hard."

He ducked his head and ran faster, wishing he could outpace this conversation, his thoughts and feelings crashing inside like the sea sprays shooting up from the rocky outcropping ahead.

"Definitely not my preferred mission destination," he said at last after they'd scrambled up and over the obstacle.

Dylan shot him a sideways glance. "It'll get better."

Except it wouldn't. Not with her in his aircraft.

"Cassie is Jeff's sister," Mark blurted and swerved around a pile of cracked-open coconuts swarming with ants.

"No shit." Dylan lost a step. "That's the blonde you were with."

He nodded and his breath came harder now, burning in his chest on its way in and out. He grabbed more water without breaking stride.

"She probably wants to follow in her brother's footsteps. I get it."

He finished his gulp and caught Dylan's shrug out of the corner of his eye. "And drive me crazy in the process."

"You like her."

Mark ran on, his lips pressed into a flat line. "I can't do anything about it." He blew out a harsh breath and for a long moment the only sound was the sea, the gulls and their feet thumping against the sand.

"Why's that?"

At Dylan's question, Mark slowed up and stopped, incredulous. He leaned over at the waist and air rasped against the back of his throat. "She's Jeff's sister. *Jeff*."

Dylan ducked under a fisherman's line and nodded at the two men it belonged to. Like many of the small groups they'd run past, they camped on the beach, trying to find a meal. "He did say you sucked for not liking *Die Hard*. But I still think he'd approve."

An agonizing flash, the feel of Cassie, warm and eager in his arms, cut through him. "I can't be with her. Dude, listen to yourself. That is Jeff's sister!"

"Why the hell not?" Dylan asked, jogging in place alongside Mark.

He straightened and stared at his friend. "Because I left Jeff."

Dylan stopped moving and broadened his stance, his feet planted so firmly in the sand he looked like he sprang from it. "We all left Jeff."

"But it was my call. I was the aircraft commander."

"Any one of us would have done the same thing. Even Jeff. Especially Jeff. He was a stickler for following procedure."

He used his T-shirt to wipe the streams of sweat running down his face, dripping into his eyes. He tasted salt on his lips. "You and I both know I should have ordered Larry to check the line again."

Dylan goggled at him. "And have run out of fuel and lost six crew members instead of one? Oh—plus our four survivors."

He opened his mouth to argue that they could have made it, but recalled Cassie's assertion that he'd had no choice. Heard his old flight instructor's admonishment to adhere to energy consumption protocol. Fuel versus distance calculations ran through his brain, the same impossible number coming up again and again. He blew out a long breath.

They wouldn't have made it.

His final memories of that moment fired through him: the horror of watching Jeff plunge back to the ocean on a snapped line. The euphoria of seeing him emerge behind a swell, okay after all. The desperate mental math that'd added up to deploying the rescue swimmer survival raft and data marker buoy before leaving his friend behind. Larry crying out *Mark, mark, mark!* as they'd marked the spot and radioed home base with the coordinates in case another asset was available to pick Jeff up.

Then, worst of all, Jeff's last confident smile as he'd waited on another swell before swimming for the gear they'd dropped.

"He had no clue," Mark muttered and began running again.

Dylan caught up. "Of course he did. Why do you think he waved?"

"He did the lasso thing."

"That was when we hoisted the last survivor in the basket."

Mark turned over the mental picture. He hadn't remembered it that way.

"He was saying goodbye. Just in case," Dylan added, his voice hoarse now.

Mark's throat swelled so tight he couldn't breathe. He'd been so focused on numbers, coordinates, ratios that he'd missed that last chance to say goodbye to his buddy...but he'd been sure they'd recover Jeff. Even when they'd returned, searching the scene for hours, then days, it'd taken a long time for him to accept they'd never get him back.

"You saved ten lives," Dylan reminded him. "If you'd made the wrong call, you would have had a helicopter upside down in the water. We all would have been statistics."

He'd made an impossible call when he'd had to and had followed protocol in the end. But that didn't make it easier to sleep at night.

Or to fly with Cassie on board. He waited for that reality check to settle in, hating the anxiety he'd feel knowing she'd be there. Jeff's sister. Facing unpredictable danger.

"Cassie's going to be our flight medic tomorrow." He didn't know why he said it since he'd had more than enough of the share-fest for the day. But the crew would find out soon enough. "She's filling in as our flight medic until Clearwater sends a replacement."

Dylan was silent for a long moment. When they reached a tall cliff, they stopped and squinted up at it.

"Then I guess you better get your head on straight sooner rather than later where she's concerned." Dylan didn't wait around for an answer before he started climbing.

Brilliant piece of advice right there. Too bad he didn't have the slightest clue how to get his head on straight when it came to Cassie. She drove him wild in a way no other woman ever had, but brought back his darkness, too.

Maybe she was right and sex would heal something for both of them—get their heads straight the way it had back in Clearwater? Sounded crazy, but hell, she was making him crazy. Why not give all that frustration an outlet?

He'd look for her tonight at the Red Cross's giveaway event. If his words didn't convince her to see reason, maybe his body could do the persuading. Make her forget this dangerous idea. It'd be a last option; one he'd avoid like hell if possible. He steeled himself for another sizzling encounter with Cassie. He just hoped the fireworks between them wouldn't blow up in his face.

8

MARK SHOVED ASIDE a green frond and emerged into the clearing the Red Cross had set up for tonight's surplus giveaway event, something the organization did to lift spirits and unload large quantities of supplies without creating long lines for the already overtaxed islanders. Despite his sour mood, one side of his mouth lifted when he spotted the "We're Alive!" sign above one of the tents pitched around the space.

That was one way to look at the situation.

Tiki torches flickered in the balmy night and bats swooped overhead. Below them, an incoming tide hissed beneath a rising moon. Then he heard it. A driving, rhythmic beat. A trio of steel drum players pounded out a tinny tune that added to the festive mood.

He eyed the long line of islanders queueing up for packages and cans of food, water and other basics. Despite their hardships, many nodded along to the music. A few even swayed and moved with the beat. The twin scents of roasting chicken and burning charcoal from a smoking fire pit beyond the trees curled through the air while overexcited children darted in and out of the crowd. Their resilience, as he'd witnessed around the world on previous disaster missions, impressed Mark. They found happiness where they could.

His eyes swerved to a flushed Cassie, who passed out cans of peaches. He hefted one of the boxes piled beside a military truck and headed her way.

Cassie's smooth fall of light hair and lush, curvy figure made his body tighten, his libido firing. In her body-hugging white T-shirt and slim khaki skirt, her fresh-scrubbed face glowing in the ambient light, her full lips stretched in a welcoming smile, she was a fantasy made real. But what made her hot as hell was the sense that she knew what she wanted and didn't hesitate to go after it in spite of everything she'd gone through.

Unfortunately, that included her wish to join him on tomorrow's treacherous mission.

His lips flattened into a tight line.

Not happening.

The Category 5 hurricane now followed a deadly figure eight pattern that slashed at Puerto Rico's leeward side before returning to swipe at the British Virgin Islands, threatening the supply route they'd established before the hurricane had jogged from its predicted trajectory and stalled. It'd be the deadliest storm he'd ever flown into and the last thing he wanted was Cassie riding shotgun.

Yet in an earlier call to COMMCEN, his command boss had confirmed what Mark had already guessed. She had the assignment unless she backed out.

He had to change that stubborn mind of hers. Maintaining his own focus once he got her alone, however, was another challenge altogether.

When she'd first seen him in Mayday's, the awareness in her gaze, the teasing, sexy game she'd played, had been like a wave of heat, burning a tantalizing path. It'd made him want her more than he'd ever wanted a woman before. And that fierce attraction had only strengthened this week, tearing him apart with as much fierceness as the hurricane that'd ravaged this island.

He rubbed his temples, feeling a headache form behind his right eye. Thinking about Cassie was like realizing, toward the end of a logic puzzle, that he'd made a mistake early on, and that there was no way to reach the solution without starting over. Without erasing everything. Without throwing out all of his assumptions.

He strode by her, and she watched, openmouthed, as he added his box to one of the piles beneath the tent. The band drummed out a percussion version of "Jump the Line," and the crowd sang along with the infectious tune. It lured the volunteer working beside her out into the now grooving crowd.

"What are you doing here?" she murmured beneath her breath, sliding him a sideways glance. Her smile didn't falter as she handed a twelve-pack of fruit to an elderly man and what looked like his daughter.

"Helping out the needy." He took an involuntary step closer, breathing in her honey-and-vanilla scent, and picked up a stack of cans. When a family of five pushed forward, he passed over the peaches.

"Doesn't that usually involve you in the air?" Her small nose scrunched and he held himself in check. Resisted the urge to kiss its tip. To kiss all of her. Every gorgeous inch.

"Let's just say, I think I can do more good here."

Their eyes met briefly before she dropped her gaze and edged away. Desire had been sparking inside him since the moment he'd spotted her, but now a pang of sharp arousal jolted him—making his crotch swell painfully.

"I don't need your help." Her shoulders rose and she held herself rigid as she continued passing out supplies.

"I don't need yours tomorrow, either." He steadfastly ignored her gasp and dropped cans into an islander's outstretched bag. The pregnant woman smiled shyly at him and a young boy clinging to her leg gave Mark a quick wave.

"This isn't the place to talk about that. Now, if you'll excuse me." She waved a can of peaches at the milling throng. "Anyone want peaches?" she called. A few of the locals stepped up. Others shook their heads and pointed to the cans they already held.

After a short flurry of takers, Cassie sighed. "No toothpaste or bread, but man, we've got peaches." A sudden gust flapped the corners of the tent and lifted her hair in a golden sheet. "And you're staring."

He jerked his gaze away. She was right. He couldn't keep his eyes off the captivating woman. As for his hands…he stuffed them in his shorts pockets to keep from taking what he wanted. And what he wanted was to haul Cassie down to the beach for a fiery tryst that'd ease the exquisite pain she caused him.

"When are you through?"

A red-headed woman he recognized—Raeanne, he thought—danced her way under the awning. "I'll relieve her. Don't see many more takers for the peaches anyway."

When Cassie frowned and started to protest, Raeanne gave her a little shove. "We got these outfits at the resort gift shop for a reason. Go have fun, or I might steal him."

She winked at Mark and, seizing the opportunity, he instinctively reached for Cassie's hand. Sparks of awareness slipped past his guard and, sure she wouldn't go anywhere alone with him, he eased her into the mass of dancers stomping to the beat.

He steered her through the writhing group until they reached its outer edge. Behind them, the rushing ocean competed with the pinging drums, a steady beat that kept time with his pounding heart. He swept her into his arms and, in an instant, his body responded to the brush of her full breasts against his chest, the tantalizing sway of her hips as they slid across his aching groin.

He grabbed for his slipping control, holding on to it barely. How to use logic on her when he could barely rationalize with himself? But he was out of choices.

"Dance with me," he groaned into her ear and, unable to resist, dragged her closer until he could feel the soft, mind-blowing length of her. His hand settled on the sweet swell of her hip.

He knew he was playing with fire, but he wanted to hold her, to feel her safe and secure in his arms. Surely he could go that far, convince her not to fly with him, and then return to his quarters.

Leave and spend another sleepless night aching for her.

She nodded slowly, her full lips pursed. The remembered feel of them, soft around his hardness, sent a bolt of heat through him as they stepped lightly to the salsa beat. She responded to the slightest pressure of his hand, followed him effortlessly, let him lead her the way he wanted to, although if he went that far they'd be somewhere alone, and with far fewer clothes on.

"I'm flying tomorrow, Mark."

He looked down at her. The moonlight turned her hair a smooth, shining silver and in the dimness, her eyes reminded him of a midnight sky. Dark and mysterious. She was sexy, so temptingly sexy. She made him want to protect her from harm, and at the same time he wanted to push her up against a wall and make her scream with pleasure.

"Conditions are deteriorating," he said gruffly, fighting his rising desire. "We'll be flying into worse weather than ever." He had to make her understand how much he needed her to stay on the ground, where he wouldn't spend every minute worrying about her.

"So it's okay for you and not for me?"

"I signed up for this."

"And so have I," she fired back.

Her eyes blazed up at him and the music slowed, each sultry note an audible caress. The thin fabric of her T-shirt slid beneath his hands as he gave into temptation and stroked her back. Her combination of strength and femininity quickened his pulse.

"I'm not changing my mind," she insisted and the husky catch in her voice was sexy as hell. Despite her rebuff, she seemed to melt against him and her head drifted down to rest on his shoulder. Her soft fingers wrapped around his, and their legs were practically entangled.

Mark fought to dredge up the arguments he'd formulated on the walk over here, but Cassie's proximity muddled his once-noble intentions. Undulating to the sultry beat, he could feel the heat of her body and her breath feathering over his jaw. Her vanilla-honey scent wove a spell around him and, yearning for a taste, his lips grazed her ear.

"I'm anticipating a lot of rescues. Injured," he forced out, striving to stay focused.

She pulled back to look up at him, her jaw set. "Sounds like I'm needed."

"Why is it so important to put yourself in danger?" he growled, his grasp tightening involuntarily as he steered her past another couple so they wouldn't be overheard. For the second time that night, he cupped her hip. Then, unable to help himself, he traced a finger across the top of her skirt, just above the elastic band of her panties.

"Because I don't want to be Cassie the Meek anymore."

He blinked and his hands stilled. *Meek* was not a word that applied to fiery Cassie.

Her eyes slid out from under his and he tipped her chin, compelling her to look at him. "You're anything but that."

Her shoulders moved restlessly and, at last, her lids lifted and her large eyes met his. "That's what everyone thinks of me back home. All my life people said Jeff was the brave one. They thought I was the quiet one, the one who needed protecting. Since I work at my family's medical office and live above their garage, I haven't done much to disprove it. No adventure and not much of a social life."

That explained her adorable, awkward flirting at Mayday's that'd turned into so much more. Releasing her hand, he skated his fingers up the satiny flesh of her inner arm, feeling the goose bumps break on her skin. They were more alike than he'd thought. She'd struggled to be more than her childhood, too.

Distracted by lingering prickles of awareness, he rocked her slowly to the beat. If his shorts grew any tighter, he wasn't sure he'd be able to keep dancing, let alone reason with her to pull out of tomorrow's mission.

"What about school friends?"

"I was homeschooled," she said, looking at their joined hands, voice softer by the syllable. "When I got bullied, my mother pulled me out."

"College?" he asked, setting his hand on the back of her neck and brushing her cheek with his thumb. She must have been besieged with would-be boyfriends. Hell. He would have been at the front of the line.

"I commuted from home."

They danced even slower now, the barest of shuffles. The kind of dancing that was more like touching to music. "Didn't you want to get away?" It bugged him that she'd been so isolated. Shut away from the world…but wasn't that, in a sense, what he wanted to do to her, too?

He shoved down the thought. Real danger loomed ahead tomorrow and Cassie wouldn't be a part of it.

"Yes. But it made my mother less anxious having me near and I'd never tried going it alone. I wasn't sure if I could handle it." As they passed a Tiki torch, it cast a warm glow on her heart-shaped face and his pulse accelerated as his focus shifted to her mouth.

"Your mother…she has…" Jeff had mentioned a condition, one that'd required him visiting his mother in the hospital. Another couple jostled them from behind and Mark clamped his arm around Cassie to steady her. Feeling her briefly pressed against him made him stifle a groan, his resistance slipping away.

"An anxiety disorder," Cassie confirmed and dropped her gaze. "She was so worried about Jeff. It was easier for me to stay and not risk her ending up in the hospital again."

"Jeff didn't agree," Mark guessed and a circuit flipped in his chest. He recalled how often his boisterous friend had cajoled and wheedled their crew into one misadventure after another. The time they'd held their own Indy 500 with commandeered mopeds, an amazing race mock-up that'd involved their base commander's office as the finish line.

Cassie nodded and her silky hair whispered across his chin. How he wanted to touch it. His hands shook, ravenous for her.

"He always nagged me to stop dithering and get out and explore." Her voice was tamped down to a whisper.

Understanding dawned. "And now you have."

"I'd never been curious to see the world until he told me about the way he saw it. The way his eyes traveled somewhere faraway when he talked about being in the air made me want to see what he did. To find out what the big draw was for him." The bruise faded out of her voice and it lifted over the sounds of the drums as they swished. "I wanted him to share that world with me."

He pulled her close, as close as he could. Like there were two of them and only one parachute. He wished he could give her back Jeff. Erase the tragedy that'd caused her so much hurt. "Now it's too late."

"No. No, it's not." Cassie's face grew animated, her eyes alight. "Riding in his helicopter will let me feel like I'm with him. Don't you understand?"

For the first time, he did. That didn't make a dent in all the rock-solid reasons why he didn't want her there.

"I can't let you on my aircraft," he said instead and he made himself look at her face, at her wide open eyes and earnest forehead. At her unbearably tender mouth as it turned down. A sweet perfume lingered as Cassie stepped back.

"Stop trying to control me. I thought being with you was different. I was different. Daring. Free. I won't be meek Cassie again."

He wanted her to be bold, too. How could he argue against that? "This isn't working," he thought out loud. His arguments weren't making any headway with her.

"No, it's not." She brushed back a strand of hair and the light gleamed on a charm dangling from her silver bracelet. An anchor. Recognition exploded in his gut. He'd been with Jeff when his friend bought a birthday gift for his beloved sister back home. Of course Cassie had worn it here. She carried her brother's memory as Mark did, had followed it into the worst storm of the century.

As if he wasn't feeling enough for her, tenderness swamped him at her dogged, gutsy determination. What was more, he desired her with a wild rush that shoved him to the edge of his control then drop-kicked him over it. The last shred of his resistance shattered.

He wanted her. Wanted the peace, the mindlessness that night in Clearwater had offered. Reason wasn't working. Not even with himself.

"I still don't want you on board tomorrow, but just dancing with you is killing me." Bending his head down, he found the beat of her pulse and he brushed his lips against it. "What if we forget everything else for tonight and just..."

Her lips curled into a sexy, sassy smile and then she veered through an opening in the shrubs beside them. What the...?

At her shouted challenge, he leaped onto the beach. Her long hair flew behind her as she raced down to the water and excitement surged. The masculine need to capture, conquer, dominate galloped through him and he sprinted after her.

Just before she reached the water, he grabbed her waist and swung her around. Their laughter rang out then slowed when he turned her in his arms and lowered her slowly along the length of his body, feeling every luscious inch of her.

Above them gulls rode the winds, screeching and calling to each other above the noise of the surf, but his mind was too filled with Cassie to notice.

He placed his hands around her face and pulled it gently to him. "You're not meek," he whispered against her mouth.

He ached. Throbbed when her lips curved and her eyes danced up at him.

"What am I, then?"

"Mine," he groaned and his mouth captured hers, feasting. He wanted to banish her hurts. Erase the pain that shadowed her eyes. He didn't know if he could protect her from the storm tomorrow, but he could shelter her tonight, comfort her the only way he knew how.

CASSIE INHALED THE sea-salt smell of Mark, the humid late-summer air silky against her skin. Despite her lingering reservations, heat rolled through her. Having such an incredibly tough, sexy man lose control over her made her feel powerful and feminine. Boldly sensual. Not meek; strong. A woman who knew her mind and got what she wanted.

Mark wasn't just someone to get her past her fears for the night, but a man who'd make her scream with pleasure.

She buried her fingers in his hair and moonlight fell around them in thick stripes. As the sea whisked across the sand, it swept up and over their feet, a warm, wet caress. Their kiss deepened and her body pulsed in awareness. Mark kissed the same way he did everything, with bold confidence and incredible skill. He slid his tongue into her mouth, his possessiveness making her moan, then pulled back, teasing, nipping at her lower lip.

Her earlier anger at him evaporated completely, replaced with a fiery hunger that made her knees weaker the longer he kissed her. It'd touched her when he'd asked questions about her past and listened carefully to her answers. His flat-out denial that she was meek filled her with the same daring she'd felt their first night together and she'd suddenly, desperately wanted to be with him again.

Mark's hands dropped to her hips, and he pulled her tightly against him, the hard length of his erection unmistakable. An answering desire pooled between her thighs. As much as she was enjoying their kiss, suddenly, it wasn't enough. The passion blossoming inside her had turned ferocious.

He must have felt the same way. Lifting his head, he said, "Let's get out of here." His breathing was rapid, his voice strained. "Find a private spot." His eyes blazed down at her, mesmerizing and intense.

She nodded. If she were any readier, they'd both be naked right now…and probably court-martialed for public indecency. Erotic fantasies spun in her mind, but they all required being alone with Mark.

Holding hands, he pulled her farther up the beach, the drumming band growing fainter, the swish hiss of the ocean the only sound besides her flailing pulse. Out of the corner of her eye, Cassie watched Mark as he moved beside her unselfconsciously, marveling at the beauty of him, of the way his muscles shifted under his skin.

After they splashed in shallow water around a rocky outcropping, Mark spun her into his arms, taking her mouth in another kiss that made every nerve ending in her body sing with pleasure. But the pleasure was edged with rising desperation. Her skin ached to be free and exposed, bared to his touch.

She moaned into the kiss, dimly aware that she was rubbing her body against his. "I want you." She tugged his lip between her teeth.

Tingles raced across her skin. Slowly, the most amazing smile stretched his mouth. Wide, knowing and enigmatic. "Come with me."

Her feet sunk into the sand, the grains colder on her toes when they reached a thickly shadowed part of this deserted strip of beach. They stopped in a small grove and the bark of a palm tree scratched against her spine when he backed her against its trunk, his hips grinding against hers. Heat crawled up her skin like a fever and her breasts flattened against the unyielding muscular wall of his chest.

She threaded her fingers in his hair and he lowered his face to hers. At the last minute, however, he shifted direction and kissed her jaw. His lips trailed down the excruciatingly sensitive line of her neck. He bit gently, then less gently, and she trembled. When his hands palmed her butt, kneading, she swallowed hard, her mouth dry with anticipation.

His kiss was deep and wet and wildly abandoned. When his hands fisted at the hem of her T-shirt, she eagerly raised her arms, ending the kiss long enough for him to lift the material over her head. They'd moved deeper still into the beach's forested ridge, away from the moon's glow. Her skin cooled from the breeze and she shivered as he outlined the swell of one breast, and her nipples contracted to even tighter points.

She shifted her weight restlessly, slick with need. It was inexplicable, how the delicate brush of his finger could trigger such an intense response. He circled one rigid tip, and she arched her back, offering herself up for further delicious exploration. But when he slid his fingers beneath the cotton of her bra, pinching lightly, it was almost too much.

She sank to the powdery sand, unable to support her weight anymore when his touch turned her to liquid. Dropping to his knees, he nuzzled the hollow of her throat, his teeth lightly scraping as he worked his way downward.

Electricity shimmied across her skin at the light rasp of thin cotton as he wrestled with the front clasp of her bra. Eyes never leaving hers, he gently unhooked her bra and drew it off. His gaze drifted lower, and his chest rose sharply as he sucked in a fast breath.

"You are beautiful," he whispered and something

about his awed tone, more than the words themselves, made her melt.

She gazed up into his glittering eyes and her fingers trembled in his hair. "So are you."

And then, with a moan of something like anguish, he slid on top of her, as hot and ready as she wanted him. His weight, wedged between her thighs as he pinned her to the soft sand, was sensual bliss.

By the time his lips reached the tip of her breast, she was breathing hard. He flicked his tongue over her, then drew her into the heat of his mouth. It was as if a current ran from his lips straight to her pulsating core.

He eased her skirt up around her waist. Her body was electric with want when his fingers skimmed up her sensitive inner thighs, then grazed over the thin fabric of her panties.

She was both frantic for him to reach beneath the flimsy barrier, to stroke her until she screamed, and more than willing to return the favor. Yet he stopped her hand when she reached for him.

"Not me. You," he murmured, his voice hoarse. He closed his eyes momentarily, his grip on her tightening. Why was he holding back?

"But—" she began but her protest evaporated when he lowered her panties, a quiver of expectation rippling through her.

His fingers parted the dewy folds, expertly finding her clit. She whimpered, moving against him urgently, reaching out blindly for him. Pleasure zinged through her body until she shuddered with it. His talented fingers worked their magic and heightened the frenzied need inside her until she almost screamed into the night.

If he'd continued, it might have been enough to push her over the edge. But he moved lower, stopping to kiss her naval then her inner thighs. And then finally, finally… "Oh!" The soft exclamation was all she could manage. Hands beneath her knees, he nudged gently, and she bent her legs, resting her feet against his shoulders. Coherent thought evaporated at the sudden, overwhelming sensation of his tongue stroking into her entrance before flicking over her clit again and again.

He continued, driving her ever higher. Her head thrashed and her heels dug into his flesh. Thankfully, only the sea and moon witnessed the cry Mark wrung from her…and if any of the partygoers overheard, she was beyond caring. Then it was as if all motion and sound stopped. Her body stiffened, a silent gasp frozen on her lips, and spasms began deep within, undulating through her, toppling into a release that exploded in frantic, exquisite sensation. Mark nuzzled her as she gripped his biceps, needing his solid presence as she shattered into a million pieces.

Unbelievable.

Mind-blowing.

Bliss.

She felt weightless, the atoms of her body floating on the breeze. When her breathing slowed, she became aware of Mark stroking her stomach and tracing the indent of her waist, the curve of her hips.

Wicked pressure slowly built again, spreading through her body, making her want him again. All of him. She lifted her head, planning to kiss him, but their gazes locked instead. Looking into his face, she knew this was the closest she'd ever felt to another person.

And even though the realization was a little scary, she was almost certain he felt the same way.

When he dropped to her side, she stretched to touch his bare thigh. The heat of that firm muscle singed her hand while the light hair of his leg rasped against her palm.

The guttural growl he made encouraged her. Called her curious hand to unclasp his shorts and touch his hard length. If his thigh had been hot, his erection was molten. And swollen. And incredibly thick.

Closing her fingers around him, she stroked up and down. Watched in rapt fascination as his eyes drifted closed at the brush of her fingertips along his shaft. A long breath hissed between his teeth when she traced the thick vein running the length of him.

She wanted him. Wanted this with an intensity that frightened her.

But she wasn't meek anymore.

With a small push, she nudged him over onto his back, tugged off his shirt and straddled him. "Cassie," he moaned and she smothered whatever he was going to say next with a deep kiss.

"Your turn," she murmured, kissing her way down his chest and abs, not stopping until she knelt between his thighs. She nuzzled him there with her cheek and placed a kiss on the tip before she slid his shorts down and off.

His body was magnificently made and his erection was no different. He stood stiff and ready, his skin richly colored there. After skimming the taut shape with her hands, she wrapped her fingers around him and drew him to her lips.

The garbled sound he made marked the first and

only time she'd rendered the controlled man incoherent. And it felt good. She lavished him with long, lingering swipes of her tongue, savoring the taste and texture. A low hum of pleasure escaped her when she took him into her mouth, mimicking the squeeze of feminine muscles all around him. His primitive, feral growl thrilled her to her toes.

Too soon, he gripped her shoulders, pulling her up to slide on top of him so that her soft flesh pressed against his hard length, so slick that all it would have taken was a slight movement of his hips to be inside her. The hard throb of him beneath her sent a hot, dizzy spike of want through her. She was more than ready for him again.

She tried to tell him she'd wanted to make him come with only her mouth. But words escaped her and she realized her whole body trembled. Her skin felt as if electricity sizzled over every inch of her. Whatever she and Mark shared, it was powerful.

Mute with hunger for him, she waited impatiently while he put on a condom. Looping her arms around his neck, she coaxed his mouth to hers then lifted her hips as he positioned himself between her thighs. He eased her down onto his hot, hard cock, filling her. She cried out as pleasure shot through her veins.

The sense of completion she felt with Mark rattled her to her core. It was a homecoming, their bodies fusing instinctively, parts of a whole rejoining at last. His taste, touch, smell, were as familiar and recognizable as they had been on their first night together. A bone-deep knowing. A rightness, a joy that only multiplied, magnified every time they touched, until there was nothing else in her thoughts but him.

He studied her through hazy, half-closed eyes and then he leaned forward and drew her nipple into his mouth. A gasp escaped her and she shuddered at the wet warmth tugging on the sensitive tip. Clutching his shoulders, she rose then sank down again. His growl of approval vibrated against her breast and he drew her nipple deeper into his hot mouth.

"Mark," she moaned, breathless. "You feel so..." Her words dissolved on her tongue, replaced with a groan when he grasped her thighs, pulling her tighter against him, embedding himself deeper.

"So tight," he whispered, grazing his teeth along her neck. "So wet and hot. Don't stop."

She didn't, taking him in long languid strokes that he met with increasing urgency, both of them straining harder for the next stroke. Her body melted for him, all around him, making each thrust more mind-blowing than the last. Her fingers plunged into his thick hair and she held him tight, kissing him frantically. All the while he plunged faster and harder, commanding the moment, steering her, guiding her hips to where he needed them. She was relieved he had control, because she'd lost hers. Her brain spun while her body rode a wave of bliss unlike anything she'd ever suspected she could feel... Their gasping breaths mingled in the still night and their bodies moved faster, wilder against each other.

Her second climax hit her like a lightning bolt, fierce spasms shaking her to the core. She cried out his name and sank her nails into his shoulders. As the waves of pleasure slowed, he held her closer, burying himself deep. His breath rasped in her ear and his rigid body told her he neared his own release, so she rocked back on her knees and increased the contact, taking him deeper still.

Pleasure spiraled through her while Mark coaxed more out of her until, at last, he shouted, a bass note of pure male satisfaction. She collapsed on top of him, limp and gloriously spent.

After a moment, his jagged breathing slowed. He pressed a kiss to her shoulder.

She closed her eyes and breathed in his masculine musk. Felt the strength of his large arms around her and the tenderness of the fingers threading through the hair at the nape of her neck. She'd never felt more safe and cared for in her life.

"We really do need to stop meeting like this," she teased to lighten the moment and motioned to the surrounding beach. She rolled over to lie on her side and her gaze met his amused topaz eyes.

One side of his mouth quirked. "I'm not complaining."

"We do our best work out here—" she trailed a finger along the curve of his bicep "—though I wouldn't mind trying out some other spots before tomorrow's mission. Just to be sure."

The sound of whirring helicopter blades cut through the quiet evening and Mark's exultant expression tightened. He sat up and leaned an elbow atop his knees, his chin resting in his cupped palm.

Uncertainty rose. "Mark?"

She stared at his tense profile as he tracked the aircraft out to sea. Why was he retreating? He must be as affected by this exhilarating moment as she was.

When her hand drifted to him, he caught it and pressed a kiss to her palm without looking at her.

"What's wrong?" she whispered, uncertainty filling her.

"Are you still flying tomorrow?" he murmured against her knuckles before his mouth trailed over them, the gentle caress making her head swim.

She pushed to her elbow when he released her hand, concern taking hold. "Yes. But that has nothing to do with tonight."

"Yes, it does." He sighed forcefully. "I shouldn't have taken you out here. Shouldn't have…" His rough voice trailed off and a muscle in his jaw jumped.

Her heart jerked. Did he regret being together? Believe he couldn't—or shouldn't—enjoy this pleasure? If so, she had to get through to him. The connection they shared hit her like a hurricane, stirring her blood to life. She wanted to comfort him. Comfort them both. Maybe if they lost themselves in each other, they would find the healing they both needed.

"Mark." She put a hand on his rigid arm. "I want to be with you."

The wind tossed the palm tree branches overhead and lifted his dark hair off his forehead. His rugged profile looked as hard as the rocky cliffs, the expression in his eyes as distant as the gleaming moon.

"I'm the last person you should want to be with," he said quietly as his eyes followed the blinking lights of another aircraft.

She sucked in the salted air and gathered her courage. "I care about you."

He turned to stare at her sharply, his expression tortured.

"If you really cared, you wouldn't fly with me."

Her stomach twisted. "You can't ask that of me."

"And you shouldn't demand that I fly you."

Silence, painful and tense, descended. At last, he nodded curtly then stood. "Let me see you home."

Knowing it'd be useless to argue against his protective nature, she dressed and followed him back down the beach to the housing units, despairing. He cared for her. Why was he denying his feelings?

"Mark, talk to me," she pleaded when they reached her quarters.

He studied her for a long moment then tipped his head and kissed her cheek. "We take off at 0600 hours. Good night, Cassie." He pivoted on his heel and strode away.

Cassie stared after Mark until he vanished from view, wishing she could conjure him back. How come she had to choose between coming to peace with Jeff's death and all the feelings she had for Mark? And why was he forcing her to choose? She'd come this far, though, and she wasn't backing down now.

9

CASSIE GRIPPED HER harness and pressed her trembling lips together as the helicopter sliced through the churning air the next day. In moments, they'd arrive on scene to rescue nine people from a floundering ferry caught on shoals off Barbuda. She needed to stay focused. Volunteering for this mission meant doing her job, honoring Jeff and seeing his world firsthand. And what a terrifying view it was… Would she be a help or a liability as Mark insisted?

Refusing to let doubt take hold, she tore her gaze off the back of his head, visible through the open cockpit. The inside of the cabin felt cramped, despite the two sliding windows on the left side of the fuselage and the helo's capacity to hold twenty-six, according to Dylan, the cheerful rescue swimmer aboard.

Her tight lungs labored to breathe the cold, damp air infused with a hint of jet fuel and salt water. Her head swam, and her mouth flooded with saliva. She felt like she was going to throw up. She bit her lip and dug her fingernails into her palms. *Steady, now.* She had to succeed, to carry on Jeff's legacy if only for one day. Complete the flight he hadn't finished. Say goodbye.

Her eyes stung and she blinked fast. Mark's anguished expression when she'd boarded this morning came to mind. Was he thinking about Jeff, too? Worried about her? It killed her that she was making a hard situation worse for him. She had to do her best on the job today and give him no reason to worry.

"CG helo, this is M/V *Sea Monarch* on Channel 16, over," said a man with a subtle Caribbean accent over the radio. The captain of the floundering ferry ship. A ringing sounded behind his transmission. His alarm system, she guessed. It set off her own warning bells as she pictured the sinking ship. She felt a sense of foreboding that had nothing to do with the worsening weather they'd headed into today. "I can see you now," the captain said. "What would you like us to do?"

The man's voice sounded strained. Exhausted. Yet he conveyed the same level of control and authority as Mark.

"M/V *Sea Monarch*, M/V *Sea Monarch*, this is CG helo 6039 on Channel 16. How do you read me?" Mark said smoothly.

"Lima Charlie," replied the captain, meaning loud and clear.

"Sir, we will be O/S in a few minutes. Please confirm the number of people on board, number of injuries, current wind direction and speed at the surface," Mark directed.

"Nine confirmed. Three non-ambulatory including a man who's pretty old and can't swim and a wounded young man with a gushing upper thigh wound," the

skipper reported. "Plus our rafts are tied up and useless."

Her stomach rolled itself into a hard ball, her pulse
skyrocketing. A femoral gash meant a patient in danger of bleeding out. She double-checked her medical
equipment, eyeing her supply of gauze pads and wraps.
It looked inadequate for the life-and-death task at hand.

"Roger, Captain. Stand by as we make a couple or-
bits. We plan on sending our rescue swimmer. Where
do you suggest we hoist him down?" Mark responded,
sounding unruffled.

"Onto the ship," the captain replied.

"Roger."

She felt the helicopter turn and craned her neck for
a glimpse of the struggling vessel.

Mark looked over his shoulder. Her heart jolted
when his golden eyes met hers briefly, something she
couldn't read flickering in their depths. "I'm going to
make two passes. You guys locked in?"

Dylan crouched at the door wearing a thick orange
waterproof suit with neon yellow sleeves, and a life
vest with an attached radio, mask and snorkel. A harness began at the top of each thigh and rose to circle
his shoulders. Black fins dangled from his right hand.
His grin transformed into a determined expression.
"Affirmative, sir."

Larry, the flight mechanic, slid open the door. Howl-
ing wind and sea spray blasted inside, the noise so
loud it drowned out the Jayhawk's rotor. The cold sting
dragged over her skin like a knife and she huddled in
her seat. Birds soared in the distance and a majestic
sea scape sprawled as far as she could see, and then the
carnage. The steel hull of the *Sea Monarch* loomed into

view. It scraped against jagged rocks, tossed around like a Tonka toy in the hands of a gorilla.

More chatter continued on her headset as the team discussed something about hoisting areas, but it became white noise as her imagination ran rampant. She closed her eyes and listened to her heart beating, the throb of blood in her neck.

At a loud swoosh, her eyes flew open. An enormous wave slammed the stern of the *Sea Monarch* and shot skyward. It nearly washed the helicopter out of the air as water jetted past the open doorway. Cassie froze in place. Even the scream that'd leaped in her throat stalled. Her heartbeat thundered in her ears. That was close.

Don't panic. Don't panic.

After a moment, Larry said, "That was a hundred feet above the pilot house."

"A hundred and sixty feet above the waterline." Dylan whistled and exchanged a nod with Larry, as if they agreed to some lethal pact.

She bit the inside of her cheek so hard she tasted blood. She was in way over her head. What if she lost it and couldn't function?

The world tilted again when they whirled in a second revolution. Then they stopped in midair, hovering. The back of the *Sea Monarch* bucked and fell in the cresting ocean.

After completing another checklist, Rob, the copilot, said, "We'll have a harness deployment of the RS with either basket or harness recoveries. If anyone requires a litter recovery, please advise ASAP, Dylan."

"As for the hoisting area," Mark cut in, "I like that

spot at the top right of the pilot house. Larry, do you see what I'm talking about?"

"Got it, sir. Concur. Plenty of room. Dylan will have to level us off before we lower him over the stanchions." As Larry spoke, he glanced at the nodding swimmer. "Sir, rescue swimmer concurs with the hoisting area."

Dylan pulled off his flight helmet and yanked up the orange hood of his waterproof suit.

After a few more challenges and responses, Mark announced, "Rescue briefing complete."

Dylan gave Cassie a thumbs-up and energy practically crackled in the air around him as he shot her a confident grin. He scooted closer to the open door and Cassie gripped her seat as the sensation of plunging out of the helicopter onto a ship in rolling seas overwhelmed her. How had Jeff done this?

Dylan donned his mask and snorkel. Larry double-checked his gear then brought him to the door. After attaching the hoist hook to the rescue swimmer's harness, he called, "Rescue Checklist Part Two complete. Ready for harness deployment of the rescue swimmer to the vessel from ninety feet."

Ninety feet!

"Check swimmer," Rob ordered.

Larry eyed Dylan as the swimmer scooted to the door's edge, his legs dangling outside. "Swimmer ready."

"Roger," Mark affirmed. Then, after a long beat of silence where everyone in the back of the cabin slid their eyes to one another, Mark barked, "Copilot, no pause button here. You ready to play ball? Your flight mech just said 'Swimmer ready'!"

"Roger," Rob blurted, sounding rushed. Was the pressure getting to him? From the forty-five-degree tilt of his head, his forward gaze at the boat's rising and falling stern, he seemed focused… "Begin the hoist."

The need to witness Dylan's descent seized her. No cowering in the back. Not today. Overriding her fear, she unbuckled herself and grabbed Larry's hand as he guided her closer and secured her with a tether.

Jeff.

This would have been his view, she thought, dizzy, as she peered over Larry's wide shoulders.

Far, far below them the sea whipped in a furious frenzy. She felt suddenly chilled as she watched wave after wave crash over the now half-submerged vessel. The crew needed to abandon ship, but couldn't.

Instead, Dylan would plunge to its slanting deck. Would Mark get him and the deckhands back to safety in time?

"Larry" came Mark's voice again. "We're going right over the sodium lights and I don't want to bash Dylan on one of those."

"Roger," Larry said, his tone crisp.

"Rob," continued Mark, "instead of lowering the swimmer down and then moving in, move in and then lower the swimmer after you pass over the lights."

"Pilot, FM. I agree. That would be best and Dylan wouldn't have to give me the level-off signal," stated Larry.

The boat pitched violently and the ocean swelled like a wild thing. Her heart clenched.

"Pilot?" prompted Larry through the ICS. Cassie saw Mark snap his face in his copilot's direction, one eyebrow raised.

"Wilco," Rob muttered at last, his tone low and uncertain.

"RS going down," Larry said. She shuddered when Dylan dropped over the side of the helicopter and began descending. "RS going down," Larry repeated. "RS halfway down."

"Big swell coming. You got this, Rob?" Mark pressed after a stretch of silence, a note of impatience in his voice.

The copilot didn't turn from the mirror outside his window.

"Big swell's hitting the stern," Rob mumbled as even less of the ship emerged through the wave. Who was he talking to? Himself? It sounded like he'd checked out.

"Forward and right fifty. Forward and right forty. Forward and right thirty," stated Larry. The helo tilted and Cassie grabbed her scuttling medical bag.

Pulse racing, she eyed Dylan, an orange speck now, dangling on a thin thread it seemed. Suddenly, he swung toward the mast.

"Whoa, whoa," Larry exclaimed, his words rapid fire. "Hold! Easy back and left, five. Back and left, five. Forward and right, five. Easy forward. Hold!"

The helicopter jittered too far sideways and plummeted, giving her that elevator stomach lurch that made whatever she'd had for breakfast—no, everything she'd eaten all week—rise in her throat.

"Whoa, whoa!" hollered Larry. The helicopter banked left then wobbled right as another geyser flew toward them. "Who's flying this thing?"

"My controls," Mark bit out suddenly. She saw his hand snake out and pry the younger officer's fingers off some kind of stick shift. Her breath stalled when they rose straight in the air. Down below, Dylan swung like a yo-yo.

"I have the controls. Continue the hoist," Mark commanded. Rob seemed frozen in his seat. Was Mark flying the aircraft alone now?

"Roger." Larry kneeled on the door edge, his arm swinging outside the helicopter, his contorted features visible behind his helmet's visor, strained. The line continued running out the door and Cassie could barely make out Dylan.

"Where's the swimmer?" Mark barked.

"RS is on board, but he's holding his arm. He clipped the sodium light when he swung during that last swell. He gave me the thumbs-up signal. I believe he's okay."

Mark's shoulders stiffened and Cassie knew he must be thinking of Jeff as she was, imagining another rescue swimmer injured or worse.

Larry announced, "Rescue swimmer, unhooked. Rescue swimmer, clear. Clear back and left, ten. Clear back and left, five."

They hovered directly over the undulating ferry boat for several heart-stopping minutes as Dylan hooked up the passengers and Larry raised and then hauled them into the cabin.

Cassie's fear dropped away when she glimpsed their ashen faces. They needed her. Even an unscathed passenger could go into shock at the narrow escape. After she assessed each person's condition, she bandaged cuts, splintered fractures and wrapped the survivors in silver Mylar blankets before guiding them to the back of the helo.

"Is skipper off?" a drenched man asked, his chest-length beard dripping. He wobbled closer and tried to peer out the door.

She put out a hand. "Sir. Please move back. We'll get everyone off safely."

Larry shot her a quick approving look over his shoulder and resumed his work.

Suddenly, her headset crackled. "Commander" came Dylan's voice. "We need the flight nurse on deck. Urgent care required for one of the crew. Arrhythmia."

She swallowed, or tried to. On deck? The ferry ground against the rocks and its deck looked as slick as an Idaho skating rink.

Mark twisted around and she caught his anguished expression. She lifted her chin. Hid her fear. Suddenly, she saw just how selfish she'd been to insist on coming on the mission. She hadn't let herself grasp just how dangerous it could be for her. How much it would hurt Mark to put her in harm's way after he'd lost her brother a year ago on a similar flight.

"We'll send the litter," he said after facing forward again, his rigid shoulders up near his ears.

"Patient's in v-fib and bleeding out," Dylan announced, sounding winded. Concern fired through her. A patient was dying on a sinking ship. She needed to get her hands on him. Stat. "He's not stable to lift. We need amiodarone now or we'll lose him."

An injectable. Beyond a rescue swimmer's EMT-Basic certification. Why she was here. But to set up an IV on a sinking ship? Her body went cold.

"We need the flight nurse, sir. We *need* Cassie, now," urged Dylan just as Larry completed another basket hoist. The flight mechanic pulled in a large woman who crossed herself repeatedly, mumbling.

Cassie checked her vitals, wrapped her in a blanket and led her to the huddled survivors in the back, her mind in overdrive. How could she upset Mark and go... but how could she stay when someone's life hung in the balance?

"Sir, survivor is in the cabin. Ready to send the basket out again," Larry spoke into his ICS.

"Stand by," she cut in before they sent that basket down without her, her voice fierce. She wasn't a passenger and had a job to do. Mark needed to see that. Trust her. "I want to help." She hurried to stock a bag with the injectable and other needed medical supplies.

"Coast Guard, our crew member's lost consciousness." This time, the ferry's captain.

"Commander?" prompted Larry.

At last, Mark rasped, "Flight nurse, you're going down. Larry, any objections?"

His order was like an earthquake. She could feel it in the center of her body, stirring her blood. She couldn't believe it. He had faith in her. Trusted she'd get the job done, despite his objections, despite his concerns. It meant everything. Larry handed her into a large metal basket and she leaned her head back against a bright orange floatation bumper.

"No, sir. No objections. Flight nurse getting in the basket. Flight nurse ready."

She gripped the basket's slick sides. Far below her the sea raged.

Her mouth worked and her eyes filled. This was it. Jeff's view, much closer than she'd ever dared imagine. More terrifying than even her worst nightmares.

"Begin the hoist," Mark ordered, his voice cracking.

Cassie screwed her eyes shut and plummeted through the water-filled air.

She'd given Mark every reason to regret bringing her along. Now was her chance to make it right.

"FLIGHT NURSE GOING out cabin door. Flight nurse going down," Larry rasped and Mark's hand tightened on the collective, his eyes glued to his gauges and monitors.

He pictured Cassie in the basket, swinging through the air. One rogue wave or gust could tear her away and he couldn't bear to lose her, he suddenly realized.

And now, he'd given the call that put her life at risk.

Mark swore beneath his breath. His worst nightmare realized. And with one order, he'd made it happen.

Regret settled in his gut, a heavy, nauseating bile. Every old emotion for Jeff and now new ones for Cassie tore up his insides, eroding them until they washed away and left the empty shell he'd been a year ago.

He stared at his instruments for a moment, but he wasn't really seeing them, not seeing anything but darkness, not hearing anything but the roaring in his ears, like the sea, or a plane right overhead.

Then Cassie's pale face swam before his eyes. His breath grew ragged, his heart beating hard enough to come through his chest. Damn it. He shook his head clear.

Stay focused.

He would get her back safely.

Would bring them all home.

"Flight nurse is below the cabin," Larry intoned. "Flight nurse is ten feet below the cabin."

He forced his fingers to relax on the collective. To stay steady. He would not lose Cassie. "Conn me in."

"Forward and right, twenty. Forward and right, fifteen. Flight nurse is halfway down."

Listening closely, he lowered the collective and shifted the cyclic right by minute degrees to get the precise measurements that'd keep Cassie away from those deadly sodium lights. If Larry didn't control the pendulum effect, if Mark was off by a foot, hell, an inch, she'd bash into them with the impact of a major car crash. Sweat streamed off his forehead and dripped into his eyes, poured down his cheeks.

Rob dropped his head back in his seat. "Sorry, sir. Would you like me to—"

"Take the radios, monitor the instruments and keep tabs of each deployment," he ground out. His copilot had lost the bubble and they'd been seconds away from dropping into the ocean. Worse, as aircraft commander, Mark should have noticed the signs. Not lost his focus. As a mentor, he should have been watching Rob like a hawk, not letting other thoughts distract him.

Time to focus.

He fought to keep a level hover, hyperaware of even the slightest movement of his Jayhawk. One wrong move could turn a controlled rescue into a disaster in an instant. Fifteen people in the water instead of the five left on the boat, the helicopter upside down in the ocean…

Cassie…

Was she frightened? God, he hoped not. His back teeth came together and his jaw clenched.

He imagined Cassie smashing into the lights. Cassie hitting a lethal spout. Cassie plummeting out of the basket. An unconscious Cassie disappearing beneath the roiling ocean…

The darkness in his head, right at the back of his skull, rose. He'd been trying to keep it at bay ever since he'd spotted Cassie striding up the airstrip this morning, but now it started to swell, to bloom.

Through the windshield, he spotted an approaching rogue wave and his pulse screamed in his ears.

"Hold!" he boomed then backed the Jayhawk off. The dagger in his heart twisted, round and round and round. "Flight nurse status?"

"Fifty feet and stable. Good work, Commander," Larry said.

The band around his lungs, if anything, tightened more. "We don't have her down, yet. Conn me in, FM."

Sitting in the seat without a mirror meant depending on the guidance of the only person with eyes on Cassie: Larry. To Mark, it felt like driving a car and trying to place the exact center of the vehicle over a quarter… blind…relying on someone who could stick their head out the door and look directly at the quarter, conning commands to either come left, come right, slow down and eventually stop directly over the coin. Nearly impossible without their level of training and skill.

He needed to rely on it now more than ever. Push out his fears for Cassie so the only noise in his head was Larry's voice, directing him.

The next few minutes lasted a year. Ten years. A hundred. How did a tortured man measure time? It expanded into an agonizing infinity where he brought them in, backed off, returned then hovered only to abort again from another violent swell.

At last, Larry announced, "Flight nurse on deck." Mark released a shaky breath. "Flight nurse getting pulled out of the basket. Flight nurse is okay. Basket clear of the deck. Clear back and left, fifteen."

Mark blew out his cheeks and his chest seemed to cave in on itself, each rib collapsing on the other. Outside, the rain spit meanly on the helo's windshield and the wind sporadically rattled the glass. Despite the fifty-five-mile-per-hour gusts from this outer edge of the hurricane, his Jayhawk held steady. He'd often thought the aircraft handled like a Lamborghini but was built like a Mack Truck. It could withstand anything.

As for him, waiting for Cassie felt like it'd destroy him.

Back at altitude and a level hover, he shifted into autopilot, a part of his brain clicking into the familiar feel and rhythms of his aircraft while another part descended into its own private hell.

How was she doing?

The *Sea Monarch*, a ferry that'd been bringing supplies and passengers from Antigua to the Virgin Islands before it got stuck in the erratic storm, tossed violently, and its forward ballast compartment was taking on water. Fast.

The ocean was picking up. He needed her, Dylan and the last passengers off now. The jagged rocks were ripping the hull open like a can opener. As long as it stayed pinned between them, they had time, but each battering wave rocked it farther off the reef. If it came loose completely, the vessel would sink in seconds.

Mark kept his breathing steady, though his heart rate picked up tempo as the ship listed and slid.

Come on, Cassie...

It shouldn't have shocked him when she'd jumped in and demanded to go down to the ship.

And she'd called herself meek… A rush of air escaped him. If she'd wanted to prove something, she'd made her point. In spades.

He pictured her the night they'd resuscitated Eloise. Her calm, professional dedication. It was exactly the right mind-set for a rescuer. In fact, she reminded him of Jeff. Her determined expression when she said she wanted to help held the same spark Jeff's had when the shit hit the fan.

And as much as this waiting drove him insane, he realized there weren't many people he'd trust more than Cassie to do what needed to be done down there.

She was competent. Focused. Brave.

Everything.

Everything to him.

A new level of respect for her grew. He'd nearly lost it when Dylan had called for the flight nurse. Not Cassie, though. She'd been fine.

He studied the tilting *Sea Monarch* and gritted his teeth. He'd gotten her down safely and he'd bring her back, too. And after that, he'd never let her go again.

CASSIE'S FEET SLID from under her the moment they touched the water-washed decking. Before she could plunge into the vicious gray sea, Dylan grabbed her arm.

"Okay?" he yelled, competing with the roaring sea.

"Got it!" she hollered, though her heartbeat and her breath ran wild. Conscious of the stinging sea spray, and the lurching deck, she huddled beside the rescue swimmer as they worked their way toward the front of the boat. The thick strap of her medic bag crossed from one shoulder down to the opposite side of her waist.

"Hurry!" Dylan shouted, glancing over his shoulder, eyes narrowing. "We've got to beat the swell."

She moved as quickly as she could, clamping down her fear. And, miraculously, adrenaline surged to fill the void. It shoved out her anxiety, empowering her as they reached a door. She jerked it open and slipped inside before another wave engulfed them.

Inside, a crew member attempted to staunch heavy bleeding from a femoral wound on a young male. His bleached skin and limp form made Cassie suck in a fast breath. A toppled AED machine rolled beside them.

"Backup battery died after the second shock," Dylan said, grim, pulling off the pads with one hand. His other arm hung by his side at an odd angle. Was it broken? If so, how was he managing this? "Didn't get any feedback." He pressed his fingers to the base of the patient's neck. "Still arrhythmic."

Cassie's mind clicked into nurse mode at the red splashed around the cabin. Could anyone survive losing this much blood? Especially one heading into cardiac arrest? She'd seen it happen, but in fully equipped ERs. Not on sinking boats that seemed to jerk the stomach out of her with each pitch and roll.

Taking over, she applied a stronger tourniquet and instructed the sailor—no, the captain, according to his badge—to keep applying pressure. Out of the corner of her eye, she glimpsed Dylan supporting an elderly man and leading him back outside to be hoisted.

With the bleeding sorted, she evaluated the man's vitals. Slow respiration. An irregular pulse and thready at best. Hands shaking slightly, she set her IV lock. She rigged the bag and assessed the patient's weight for dosage. He looked to be around one-eighty, but with his blood loss…

She was so lost in thought that when the next wave hit, she flew across the narrow room and bashed against a wall. A horrible scraping sound, metal against stone, rose around her and the boat seemed to swell beneath her feet.

"Okay over there?"

She scrambled upright and gave the ferry captain a quick nod, ignoring the dull ache blooming up her arm and shoulder. But how much more time before the next swell? She measured out 300 mg of amiodarone and began a rapid IV push. When water crept beneath the door and lifted the man's hair off the floor, she didn't pause. If they went under, she'd go down fighting.

Dylan appeared again. "Can we transport him? Litter's outside."

She shook her head. The hemorrhage had slowed but any big movements and he might bleed right out until she had that better controlled. More important, she needed to stabilize his heart rhythm. "You need to take care of your arm."

Dylan shrugged, looking pumped instead of in pain. "Just a flesh wound. Be right back." He looped his good arm around a limping teenager and headed out.

At last the pilot house was empty except for the captain, Cassie, their victim and the rising sea that now lapped around the downed man's ears. Cassie's lungs froze as she kept checking her patient's erratic pulse. Three more minutes before she could give another push. Two…

"We've got to go," the captain shouted at her over

the rushing wave that tumbled them sideways again. The boat angled back slowly, listing heavily. "She's coming apart."

She shook her head. "I won't risk it. He needs another push." After a 150 mg injection, she held the man's cold wrist. Her heart rate sped until, at last, she felt a small, steady pulse against her index finger. A fierce rush of joy pounded through her. "Pulse is stable."

"Good work." The skipper shot her a look that said every brave thing she'd ever thought about Jeff.

Dylan burst through the door. "Gotta go!"

He hoisted their victim and together they stumbled into sea surge that rose above her knees. *Good God.*

The litter swirled in the water and drifted their way. Dylan reeled it in, loaded the injured crew member and signaled for Larry to lift it.

"You're next." Dylan pointed at the captain, who shook his head.

"I'm the last off." For the first time, she noticed that the back of his head was bleeding.

"No, you're not. You need medical attention," she called over the raging water just before it crashed over them. It lifted her off her feet and nearly swept her over the side before she snatched one of the boat's lines.

Dylan appeared and hauled her on deck, the veins on his good arm bulging. "Hang on!" he screamed over the shrieking wind. "I'm hooking up the skipper, then I'll lift you. Got it?"

She nodded, lips shaking. Yes, she could swim. In pools. The shallow end, specifically, since that was all her mother had allowed. Still, she could tread water. And she was wearing a life preserver, she reminded herself. Her legs bowed as she fought to stay afoot when another swell rushed over them. Smaller this time. Which meant—what? An even bigger one next? The one that'd completely take them down?

"Abandon ship! Abandon ship!" Dylan hollered as the boat shuddered and lifted before crashing smack down on its side.

She leaped into the whirling water and kicked hard against the sucking drag, her life preserver no match for the powerful force. Coughing and spitting out salt water, she flailed, trying to keep her head above the enraged ocean intent on swallowing everything. Including her.

Dylan reached her, cradled her head in his arm and began kicking them backward, hard, keeping her mouth above water. When she looked skyward, she didn't spot the Jayhawk and her heart seized.

Had they lost them?

Would she and Dylan drown?

"Keep kicking!" urged Dylan and she put her shaking muscles into it. The injured swimmer wasn't giving in and neither would she.

Several seconds, minutes, hours seemed to pass— she'd lost count—as she and Dylan battled the waves before, miraculously, a rescue strop dropped directly in front of them.

In a flash, Dylan had them hooked. Air whistled around her as they swung toward the helicopter. Larry snatched them into the cabin the moment her toes grazed the side of the aircraft.

The cabin door slammed shut. She blinked at the crying, shaking and staring survivors and her thoughts tumbled. A deep shudder started in her gut and rattled her to her toes. She pressed her hand against the Jay-hawk's side, not trusting that she really was out of the water and here.

Safe.

When she caught sight of her v-fib patient, she crouch-walked to his side as the helicopter wheeled then sped. What a relief to see the IV still attached to the litter.

She checked his vitals and tourniquet.

Stable. Critical, but stable. Hopefully enough to get to the airport then medevac to a major hospital.

A life saved. One for her and how many more for these extraordinary men? She looked around the cabin, deeply impressed as Dylan shrugged off any fussing over his dangling arm and began checking passengers alongside her.

"Swimmers." Larry rolled his eyes at Dylan. "Crazy sons of bitches."

"Or looking for some shirt candy," put in Rob with a sheepish glance behind him.

"It's an Air Medal for sure. You, too, Cassie, if you were in the Coast Guard." Dylan's cocky grin was firmly back in place.

Her gaze swerved to the cockpit and a spark, like the shock off an electric fence, went through her as she met Mark's eyes. They stared at each other for a moment before he turned back, but the glimpse of his anguished expression tormented her. Made her want to reassure him she was fine. Not scared after all, she suddenly realized. She'd been so intent on her job, so focused on her survival, that she hadn't been meek at all.

The change swept through her skin, whirling in the

vast spaces between her atoms, reconfiguring her into someone else—or perhaps, as Jeff had pointed out, the person she was meant to be all along.

_10_

MARK RAPPED ON Cassie's door and stared at the stubbornly shut entrance. The wooden door felt entirely too solid for his liking. He didn't want barriers between them. Not after nearly losing her this afternoon.

Where was she?

After finishing his flight paperwork, he'd headed straight to the field hospital. While Dylan, who turned out to have a broken arm and a concussion, joked and flirted with nurses, Cassie was nowhere to be found.

After a quick shower, he'd spent an hour scouring the staging area, returning to her room three times because, as well as she'd done today, he'd been sure she'd be rattled enough to head to her quarters.

Shouldn't she be in bed, as wrecked by her close call as he was? She was strong, but she wasn't inhuman.

He needed to hear her heartbeat. Lose himself in her body. Remind himself that they were both alive and that the nightmare looping in his brain wasn't real. He'd been powerless to stop her from going overboard.

What if he'd lost her?

The horrifying image of Cassie leaping off the sinking ship, her head disappearing beneath a thirty-foot swell, slammed into his brain like a gunshot. Each time he thought of it, every second since he'd landed the helicopter, he died inside.

He closed his eyes and slumped against the door-jamb, trying and failing to shake the gut-ripping memory. How had he given the order to lower her to the deck?

The question was a hot poker prodding his searing chest. He'd vowed to protect her and had nearly let her die. Voices down the building-length concrete veranda grew louder, followed by someone knocking on a neighbor's door. An excited exchange rose then fell as the group disappeared. Reunited.

His head sunk to his hands and he stood, hunched his back braced against the rising night wind. An aircraft engine whined in the distance. He felt damaged and raw, his nerve endings exposed.

Today's mission had gutted him. Dylan's broken arm. The leg amputation of one of the survivors. And Cassie. How fragile she'd looked as the ocean dragged and tossed her. His breath had spun out of him and it'd taken every ounce of his training not to let go of the controls and dive into the water after her.

"Hey. Are you okay?"

He glanced up at Cassie's red-headed friend. Rae-anne. She shoved back wavy hair and peered at him, her thin eyebrows meeting above her nose, her metal earrings catching the overhead light. At her anxious expression, he squared his shoulders. Gritted his teeth. As for talking, that was beyond him so he simply nodded.

When she jerked a thumb over her shoulder, her

keys jangled. "Cassie's at the canteen if you're looking for her."

"The canteen?" The words burst out of him, overloud.

Raeanne smoothed down a yellow tank top that didn't quite meet the top of her jeans. "I just came from there to get my sweater. If you wait, we can—"

"Thanks!" he called over his shoulder as he jogged down the porch's five steps. His boots ground against the pebbled oceanside walk to the makeshift hangout created from one of the resort's bars. What the hell was Cassie doing there?

Adrenaline buzzed through him like it always did during and after such touch and go rescues. He wanted to find Cassie before that energy jolt disappeared and he spiraled so far down that he might not make it back.

Why was she out celebrating?

Didn't it bother her that she could have shared her brother's fate? This wasn't a time to minimize what'd happened. If anything it should be a serious wake-up call.

It'd put him on high alert. When he'd confirmed his new AST3 had arrived for tomorrow's mission, he'd breathed a sigh of relief. Never again would he go through that hell with her.

He shoved clenched hands into his pockets and picked up his pace. Above him the sky was dark and still, the waves bobbing politely, tiptoeing their way across the beach. A couple of servicemen jerked back into leaf-stripped hedges as he barreled by, nodding in greeting without stopping.

Damn it. He needed her. Now. Desperation shredded his insides, ravaged his guts. The relief he should have felt when she'd emerged from the water, strapped to Dylan, eluded him. Once he had her in his arms, whole and warm, he wouldn't let go until he assured himself she was okay.

He jogged down to the open gate that led through a paved terrace, its whitewash worn and blistered with rust-colored lichen. Her throaty laugh stopped him in his tracks. Just ahead, the bar sign's chains swung from the mostly bare thatched roof of the hut-like structure. USCG and Red Cross personnel surrounded a square outdoor bar. A couple of ambitious islanders poured shots of rum into plastic cups and passed them to the cash-waving, off duty crowd.

Of all the places he'd imagined finding her, this was the last.

Looking impossibly sexy in a short, fitted blue dress that showcased long, curvy legs, her shining hair curling just above the tops of her full breasts, Cassie had a crowd of admirers. When one of them brayed something, she tossed her head back and laughed, swatting the guy's arm playfully.

The sight stopped him in his tracks. It...changed everything about her. Until that moment, he hadn't realized just how wistful her gaze had been. It was as if someone had flipped on a switch. Confusion and agitation warred inside Mark's chest.

Didn't she understand that she'd nearly lost her life? How precious it was—she was—to him? Then again, how would she know? He could barely admit those feelings to himself. Tight knots squeezed hard in the pit of his stomach.

As Mark approached, Larry called out.

"Here's the man of the hour! Cheers to the commander for getting all of our asses home today."

A hearty "Yeah!" rose from the group and Cassie's eyes sparkled at him before she downed her drink.

"Have a shot." Larry thrust a cup into his hand. A sharp, rich smell wafted from the sloshing clear liquid. It was tempting, given they had twelve hours of R & R before they were wheels up again. But it wasn't even close to what he wanted. Eyes locked with Cassie's, he downed the drink and set the empty cup on the bar with a thanks, nerves rippling through him.

"Cassie? A word."

A hush descended on the chattering group and gazes swerved between him and a now sober-faced Cassie. Without looking away, she handed her cup over.

"Be right back," she called. Once they rounded a corner, she slid her soft hand into his. The sweet familiarity of her touch went through him like a shock.

He hustled her behind the canteen, into what'd been a garden Mark guessed. Empty concrete pads marked where benches had stood. Uprooted and mangled bushes lay on the spongy ground. After several minutes of striving to slow his thoughts, he jerked to a halt before a mermaid fountain. Moonlight drifted across Cassie's delicate features. How was it possible that she stood here in one piece, alive, after her narrow escape?

He raked a hand through his hair, drinking in the sight of her. "Do you have any idea how close I came to losing you?"

Then, too impatient to wait for her answer, he kissed her so hard their teeth collided, kissed her for each and every second that he'd spent scared out of his mind up in the air today.

Her body trembled against his when he nipped her bottom lip, and she moaned inside his mouth, whispering his name, her head falling back and spine arching. The scents of honey and vanilla wafted from her neck, drugging him. He kissed the warm leap of her pulse at her throat, savoring the feel of her, safe and alive, the proof at his lips. Hands tangling in her hair, he combed through the silk, pressing her closer. Closer. Her hips fit to his, breasts molding against his chest.

He kissed her harder now, wanting more. He couldn't get enough, would never be able to get enough. He wanted her beneath him, wanted to bury himself deep inside her until he drove away his demons. Not just with his own release, but hers, again and again and again.

"I know how close that was," she said when he stopped to let them catch their breaths, their mouths inches apart, their foreheads pressed together. She tipped her head back and lifted glittering eyes to his, her expression electric with the same adrenaline that jittered through him. "But I can't process it."

He skated his fingertips up and down her bare arms and his cock swelled at the satin feel of her. "Once the extra energy wears off, you'll come down hard." And he'd be there to reassure her that she wouldn't be in danger again.

She shook her head. "I won't let myself feel afraid anymore."

His grip tightened on her arms and he dragged her close, trying to calm the storm in his head. "You could have died." A deep shudder ripped through him.

Her lips moved along his neck, firing nerve endings

to life. "But I didn't." She moved closer still and plastered her body to his, her eyes drifting closed.

"Come to my room," he murmured against her cheek, his body tense, willing her to agree.

Her eyes opened, bored into his, and then she smiled, a heady half smile that spoke of her own desire. She wanted him the way he wanted her. She stood on tiptoe and kissed him with a passion that made him rock hard. "Yes."

He kissed her backward, steering them both where they needed to go, only breaking the contact when he saw someone else on the path to his quarters. Then he tucked her under one arm and hurried her into the shadows and—finally—into his room, where he planned to make every nerve ending that had been at risk today scream.

Inside, he pinned her against the door, his hands reaching around her back for her dress's collar-to-hem zipper. The movement incited something in her, wresting a cry from her throat as she rubbed her breasts over his chest and broke his kiss to nip his shoulder. The zipper's teeth came apart when he tugged it all the way down. The dress separated then pooled at her feet. He freed the hooks on her bra and slid the soft cotton off her shoulders.

The warm silk of her skin fried his brain cells, robbing him of any thought save having her. All of her. His hands roamed across her body, palming her firm ass, tracing her narrow waist, skimming her taut stomach, then rising to cup her full breasts before moving on again, never settling in one place long enough to soothe the ache building inside.

He stopped only long enough to remove the rest of

her clothes. The soft mewling sounds she made in the back of her throat assured him she craved his touch every bit as much as he craved the feel of her skin beneath his hands.

Her eyes went wide as his fingers dug into the soft globes of her ass and boosted her up. "I need you. Now," he growled, impatient, desperate to feel her against him, his control held by the thinnest thread.

Cassie wrapped her legs around his hips, and the tantalizing softness of her, rubbing his rigid cock, made him groan. Filled him with staggering need.

As she bounced against his sensitive tip, he carried her to the bed and laid her on the mattress. He whipped off his shirt and balled it up, tossing it in the general vicinity of the television. As he quickly stripped off socks and boots and fumbled with his belt, she rose up on her elbows.

With her hair tousled, her warm eyes gazing up at him through lowered lids, she was the sexiest woman he'd ever seen. The need to bury himself inside her whipped through him, punishing and relentless. She nearly sent him to his knees.

Grabbing a condom from his bedside drawer, he ripped off the foil wrapper and began unfurling it over his erection. His fingers trembled, the burning need to join with her making him clumsy. Off his game.

But this wasn't some game.

Not even close.

"Let me," she whispered. She rolled it down his length. Her teasing touch unleashed a mad fury that howled inside and untethered his last shred of willpower.

The bed dipped as he slid over her. His legs spread

hers. This was what he wanted, what he'd tried like hell to deny, what he'd crave tomorrow even more for having surrendered himself today. Only Cassie drove him to this level of distraction.

He yanked his gaze up to her eyes to find her staring at him with equal intensity, her emotions bared. He should look away. Focus on sex. But some sort of communication happened without his realizing it, an understanding that went beyond mind-blowing orgasms. He closed his eyes to shut it out, knowing he was too late.

He lowered his mouth to her breast and drew on the taut nipple, savoring the taste of her on his tongue. She wriggled and writhed and guided his hand between her legs, inviting him inside.

In one swift thrust he filled her to the hilt. Her wanton gasp echoed in his ear and he groaned at the warm clench of her flesh around him. So good. So right.

He battled to hold back, waiting for her to adjust to the feel of him, sure that he'd explode if he didn't regain some control.

When she raised her hips, he whispered, "Don't move," willing her to understand his need to take charge after such a chaotic day. To command this moment. Master himself and the wild feelings for her that spiraled through him. He brushed his mouth against the shell of her ear. His tongue traced its outline and made her whimper. At her back, his fingers splayed, widening, then contracting. He wanted to hold her tight and banish the sense that she'd slip away from him again.

"Mark, please," she begged against his mouth and his mind emptied of everything except the way she made him feel.

Hot. Greedy. Ravenous.

His tongue thrust deep inside her mouth, demanding. She parried and groaned, her eyes flaring wide with longing for him. Her fingers stroked his shoulders and his muscles bunched at her touch, his body taut with anticipation.

She writhed beneath him and he could feel her heart beat, matching the frenetic tattoo in his own chest. He said her name a million times, as if to remind himself that she was here, whole and alive, and the world that'd tried stealing her from him had failed.

Their kisses grew deeper, more urgent. If he didn't give in to this insistent need soon, he'd explode. He broke off, his hands on her face. Her flushed skin mirrored the heat spiking through him, her nipples tinged with color. She was an incredible sight. Her lips were plump and wet; her panting breaths warm on his chest.

"Don't leave me." The unconscious words ripped out of him too fast to take back. His hands slid to her breasts now, cupping and massaging, his breath thick in his throat.

"I won't," she panted, winding her arms around his neck, holding on to him as if she'd never let go. The tender gesture stirred something deep within. The honey scent of her skin was intoxicating. He inhaled deeply.

Cupping her deliciously curved ass, he angled her hips, withdrawing slightly, then thrusting inside all over again, striving for the mind-blowing rhythm that would make him forget this day and the ever-strengthening bond that anchored him to her.

In a state of frenzy, he lifted her legs onto his shoulders to accommodate his blistering pace, giving him deeper and deeper access. He willed her to understand his need to forget. To lose himself in this.

But she only kissed him and tantalized him, her swiveling hips an erotic tease that both set him ablaze and fueled his sense of rightness with this uninhibited woman. Her obvious pleasure was a massive sexual windup that blasted through the day's torment, shattering it with intense, scorching excitement.

Her lashes fluttered closed, her breath coming in short gasps each time they crashed together. Their movements turned fierce and urgent as they rocked. Pressure mounted inside him in some exquisite balance between pleasure and pain. Yet he held himself back, wanting her to reach her peak first.

The covers scrunched and whisked beneath them as he bucked within her, filling her completely. He could feel her heart pounding against his chest—or was that his heart? He wasn't sure anymore if there was a distinction.

"Mark. Yes!" she shrieked suddenly, her primal cry loud in the small room. Her head twisted from side to side and her inner muscles gripped him harder still, rippling around his cock, a tidal wave sweeping over him. He groaned in blissful agony and let go, exploding inside her, his release coming in an endless chain of spasms.

Holy hell.

When his breathing returned to normal, he enclosed her in his arms, pulling her to him so tightly that their bodies felt welded together. As he cradled her, the unmoored sensation that'd gripped him since she'd plunged into the sea faded. She was okay and, therefore, so was he. The thought was unsettling.

He watched her eyes open, her gaze unfocused, mouth curving. "That was incredible. You're incredible," she said softly.

"I could say the same." He kissed the top of her head, let his fingers rest in her tangled hair. A perfect peace had descended on him, spreading to his very bones. "And I have a pretty high score to live up to."

She shifted in his arms and her eyes settled on his face, considering, a teasing smile tugging at the corners of her mouth. "I didn't think you could beat that last one, but you just might have…"

"Might?" He kissed her collarbone, her chin, the space where her jaw met her ear, and he felt himself hardening again. She radiated heat like a warmed-up engine. "We'll see about that…"

Sometime later, he rested his head in the curve of her neck, listening to the distant rolling timpani beat of the wind and incoming thunder. He wasn't sure how long they lay there together, as if each wished to absorb the other through their skin, a marrow-deep connection that filled him with both happiness and unease.

Sex with Cassie went beyond physical. Tonight, it'd reached an emotional level that he couldn't deal with right now, not with his future uncertain, his need to make a decision on grounding himself after today's mission. He'd taken charge of the flight, had managed to get them all home safe. But as mission commander, he was responsible for overseeing every aspect of the operation and that included mistakes. If he'd been clearheaded, he would have noticed Rob's struggle to stay calm, would have taken over before his trainee checked out and nearly scuttled them into the sea, potentially losing all lives.

Cassie.

It scared the hell out of him how much Cassie had come to mean to him in such a short amount of time. But in a few days, she'd fly home. What could they figure out, relationshipwise, with so little time? Best to go their separate ways and not entangle her in his mess of a life, no matter how tempting she was. Fate had brought them together for this short time, but that was all it could be. All a man in his position could offer.

He heard the sounds of her even breathing in his ear and felt himself slip, at last, into welcome oblivion.

RAIN TAPPING AGAINST glass woke Cassie hours later. She opened her eyes wide, briefly uncomprehending in her half slumber how she could have ended up in the same bed as this man. When she remembered, she reached for Mark, linking her arms languorously around his neck, squinting in the gloom.

What time was it? Five in the morning according to her cell phone screen on the bedside table. Since they had the medical aid response in hand now, she'd been ordered to get some much-needed rest and had the day off. No need to get up. Thank. God. Her body ached in a delicious way that reminded her of everything he'd done to make her scream with pleasure last night.

She'd never felt so powerful, so liberated and turned on as she felt with Mark. Their steamy lovemaking un-locked another part of her—the strong, decisive woman she'd glimpsed while flying yesterday's mission, who could control and lose herself at the same time. Never would she return to being the person who made easy, safe choices or, worse, none at all.

Mark shifted slightly in his sleep, and she tilted her

head so she could place a soft kiss on his forehead. He answered with a murmur, and Cassie's heart clenched with gratitude. *Thank you*, she told whoever might be listening. *Thank you for giving this to me.*

Mark stirred and opened his topaz eyes. For a fraction of a second, they were blank, uncomprehending, and then they warmed and he smiled.

"Hello," she murmured, brushing a finger along the sexy stubble of his jaw.

It rattled her to think how much she'd come to care for this strong, determined pilot with a big heart. A man who'd saved her in more ways than one.

"Come here." He pulled her to him and lavished her neck with lazy, toe-curling kisses. Surrendering herself to the sensation, she closed her eyes, feeling her heart flicker inside her chest. "Cassie…"

She shushed him with a finger. She didn't want words just yet; she wanted to soak in the moment, their bodies warm, tangled and sprawled.

His fingers threaded through the strands of her hair, carefully combing them, before fanning them out on the pillow. Then he raised himself up on an elbow and rubbed his eyes. His hair stuck up on one side. Despite his disheveled state, the man was living art. His shoulders were broad and strong, his chest dusted in dark hair. His torso tapered to an impressively ridged six-pack that she would have assumed was airbrushed if she'd seen it in a photo.

He kissed her lightly on the nose. "Are you hungry?" he asked, his low voice vibrating against her cheek.

"A little."

"On it."

When he started to slide off the bed, she held tight.

She relished the closeness of him, let herself be consumed by the simple pleasure of his skin against hers—strong, sinewy male flesh, its musky scent and smooth, firm textures. She liked the strangeness of him, the strength of their combined bodies, the way his size, while intimidating, didn't make her feel weak. The way his desire emboldened her.

"I don't think I have the energy to eat," she groaned, feeling the languid heaviness in her limbs.

He chuckled, low and sexy. "Having trouble keeping up?" He grazed the soft plane of her belly with his fingertips, making it contract.

His chest hair was soft beneath her fingertips. "On second thought, maybe I do need sustenance."

He stepped out of bed, and she couldn't help staring in appreciation at his firm backside as he strode away. A metallic scrape sounded. Then, a moment later, he eased close again, holding, of all things, an open can of peaches.

The sweet smell made her nose tingle. "Where did you...?"

"I have connections." He shot her a meaningful look and she laughed softly, remembering the night she'd practically begged people to use up her surplus supply... the incredible night on the beach, Mark's mouth hot and insistent on her.

She shifted, pleasure pulsing in her core. Really? Did he make her this insatiable? Apparently. But she wanted to know more about him than his skills in bed and in the air. She needed to understand if the raw emotions she'd glimpsed in his eyes earlier, the deep connection they'd shared, was more than her imagining.

He glided a peach slice over her lips so that its rich syrup dripped into her mouth.

"Mmm," she moaned when he slid it into her open mouth and the fruit's tart, summery taste exploded on her tongue. Her stomach growled. She was ravenous. Out of the corner of her eye, she glimpsed Mark's rippling abdomen and another craving took hold, one she'd postpone, tempting as it'd be to have him moving inside her again right now.

He propped himself up on one elbow and touched another piece to her mouth. He enticed her with the scent as he skated the peach slice along her lower lip, his gaze riveted there.

A cold drop of juice wove down her chin. Before she could reach to wipe it off, Mark bent over her and licked it away with his tongue. The movement happened so quickly she might've thought she'd fantasized it if not for the way her flesh sizzled in that one moist spot.

He held the slice above her mouth, his voice low and inviting in her ear. "What do you think, Cassie? Ready for more?"

The wicked gleam in his eye left little question that he asked about more than just peaches. All her nerve endings leaped to life, as if every last one of them thirsted for his touch.

"I'm ready." Arching her neck, she lifted her head to the dangling fruit and sucked it from his fingertips, the rich juice sliding down her throat as she chewed.

Mark watched her like a starving man and, unable to help herself, she licked her lips to seek out every last bit of liquid, wanting to taste him, too. She cupped his cheek in her hand, tilting his head so their eyes met.

"Your turn," she murmured. She got to her knees, and a low moan escaped him as his heated eyes ran over her body.

"No." He eased her back down to the pillow.

"Why?"

"I want to indulge you." When she started to protest, he placed a finger to her mouth. "Let me, Cassie." The hoarse tone of his voice reminded her of the unchained emotion she'd glimpsed in his eyes when he'd found her at the canteen. The desperate fury of his lovemaking.

"Do you know how close I came to losing you?" he demanded. Had her close call yesterday affected him this much? Shaken him? Did that mean he cared for her, too?

Regret twisted in her gut as she sampled the next peach slice he fed her. Had she been wrong to force her presence in his helicopter? To push him? Clearly, he walked a tightrope. She'd only been thinking of herself and her demons and hadn't listened to Mark.

"Thirsty?"

Before she finished nodding, he'd crossed the room, grabbed a couple of bottled waters and stretched out beside her. He unscrewed the cap and lifted it to her mouth.

"Mark. I can do it," she protested. He surrendered the plastic container and they eyed each other as they sipped. "Why are you doing this?"

"You look hungry. Thirsty." He ducked his head.

"I mean *this*." She gestured between their bodies.

After an awkward silence, he said, "I wanted to. Want to."

"Me, too." Their eyes met for a heart-stopping moment before she said, "And I'm sorry about yesterday."

A muscle jumped in his jaw and his gaze jerked away from her. "You're sorry?"

She blinked at him in surprise. "Yes. I insisted on flying with you."

"And you nearly died on my watch."

"That was my risk to take."

"And you did a great job."

His words were like sparklers that sizzled inside Cassie. "Thank you. I—uh—actually enjoyed it," she admitted, knowing it sounded crazy to say almost losing your life was fun...but that moment, the rush of saving others, was incredible.

He tossed back a long gulp of water then said, "But you don't know what SAR is really like on a day-to-day basis."

"Then tell me."

He drained his bottle and lobbed it into the trash can. "It's not just a job. It's your life. No. It's thousands of other people's lives that you're charged with protecting. Rescuing. Ask me how many saves I've made and I couldn't tell you. But I know exactly how many I haven't because they're the ones that keep you up nights."

She instantly thought of Jeff but pressed the thought back into her mental scrapbook to save for later. Not now. Not with emotions running this high.

"Let's talk about something else," he murmured, his voice more in control again. Reaching for another peach, he touched it to the hollow of her throat and slid it down to the top of each breast before circling each nipple with its wetness. Heat flared between her thighs and she could feel herself growing as slick as the peach he teased her with. "Or not talk at all," he bent over and whispered in her ear.

Her breath hitched and she tried remembering the square root of one hundred and ninety-six. Anything to stop her from giving in to the molten desire Mark ignited.

"Why did you join the service?"

He stopped nibbling her earlobe and his warm breath rushed across her sensitive skin. "You're not letting up."

"I want to know you."

His eyes delved into hers. "I joined because I wanted to be one of the good guys."

"Weren't you already a good guy?" His answer caught her off guard. She would have thought he'd joined for adventure. The thrill. Status...

"I wanted to be different than..." His voice dipped and she turned her head so that their noses touched.

"Than...?" she prompted, trying and failing to meet his eye.

"My dad was in jail." He jerked out of bed and strode to the sink. He turned the knobs then swore softly when no water gushed from the faucet.

She studied the tense curve of his back as he leaned against the counter, wanting to comfort him.

"I'm sorry."

After a moment, he sat by her side and cradled her hand, turning it over in his palm. "Don't be. He deserved to be there." Bitter sediment ran along the bottom of his voice. "Armed robbery." A laugh that sounded anything but amused escaped him. "I never understood why my mother forgave him. Some things aren't forgivable."

She ducked under his arm and crawled onto his lap. He pulled her head to his chest and she felt the steady thud of his heart against her ear.

"You're one of the good guys, Mark."

He was silent. She held both sides of his face and gazed up at him. "Don't you believe that?"

The infinite sadness in his eyes arrowed through her heart. "I believe in this…"

He lowered his lips to her neck while his hands cupped her breasts in a provocative torment that stopped her torrent of questions. He grew harder beneath her ass and she felt an answering rush of wetness deep within.

"I need you," he rasped against her neck and she seized his shoulders, straddling his legs. He gazed into her eyes, seeing more deeply inside her soul than anyone had ever bothered to look. In that moment, Cassie knew they had gone too far, or she had, her heart leaping down a path she wasn't sure Mark could follow.

"I need you, too," she gasped when he scooched her up farther on his lap and her slick core slid against the hard tip of his penis. He hauled her closer still, so that they were pressed together. She swiveled her hips, grinding against him, hearing the way he sucked in his breath, loving that his reaction to her was every bit as strong as hers to him. When his hands traveled over her, the hungry feel of them on her skin ignited her like a match to gunpowder and she couldn't wait any longer to feel him inside of her.

This time when he made love to her, he did so slowly. He spoke to her body with his own. She felt her inhibitions fall away. The rest of the world slowed and closed in, until it was just the two of them, their breaths coming in short gasps, the air around them a bright light that blotted out everything, dissolving them both.

Afterward, she watched the steady rise and fall of Mark's chest, her mind in too much tumult to let her rest, too. Mark stirred up powerful feelings she'd never experienced before. His passion set her on fire, but his tenderness melted her completely. He'd said he needed her. Was that in the physical sense only?

There was only so much time left before they parted and she might never see him again.

For her this thing between them felt real.

For Mark…she hadn't a clue. He could make love to her until she couldn't see straight, but it was obvious that she reminded him of the painful save he hadn't made. Would he ever want a future with her when the specter of Jeff still rode in his aircraft?

11

MARK BATTLED TO stay atop the raging ocean. The wind hissed in his ears, sea spray stung his nose and he gagged on briny water. A giant hand seemed to snatch at his thrashing legs, the pulling sensation of another oncoming swell. His pulse hammered and he swiveled in every direction. He squinted through the mist-filled air until he spotted a bright orange suit bobbing in the seething water.

Cassie!

Only forty yards away.

He kicked hard, his arms cleaving the surface. Then a mountainous wave crashed over him and dragged him under, twisting and turning him in somersaults. When it let go, he lost his orientation in a murk of blue. Where was the surface?

His lungs burned and he fought to keep his head. *Stay calm. Think. Spot which way the current flows the way your training taught you.* Yet the water swirled in too many directions at once. When he spotted floating debris to his left, he twisted in that direction, and shot that way. If he guessed wrong, he'd die. And so would Cassie. He had to get it right for both of them.

A moment later, his head emerged. He spit out a mouthful of salt water before dragging in a long breath. Had he lost her? Eyes stinging, he scanned the churning water until he spied her again even farther away. Adrenaline surged. Yet when her bright head turned, he glimpsed someone else's face. Jeff! Mark watched in horror as another wave yanked his friend under and he disappeared.

MARK JERKED UPRIGHT in bed. His chest pounded, his body slick with sweat. There was a faint ringing sound in his ears. He shook his head, trying to get rid of it. After blinking up at the ceiling for a few dazed moments, full consciousness returned.

His muscles clenched as he gazed down at the woman who slumbered beside him. Even puffs of air escaped her parted mouth and her golden hair curled around her sleep-flushed face. He balled his hands to keep from reaching for her. It'd only been a nightmare. That was all.

Still, the memory of her brave jump into the ocean yesterday chopped him straight in his windpipe. Amazing how she hadn't been cowed during that volatile, deteriorating situation. She'd done her job well and hadn't let her emotions get to her. No. Cassie wasn't meek. She was strong, a fighter. What's more, she'd rocked his world last night, her passion and the depth of emotion in her eyes mirroring his own feelings.

And it scared the crap out of him.

How could he explain that once he'd gotten to know Cassie everything he'd known, everything he'd believed, had been sucked away like someone pulling a rug from under him? How could he tell Cassie she couldn't risk her life when it would endanger everything he gave a damn about in this world?

He couldn't. Not when he could barely figure out where his head was at, let alone his heart. Yet somewhere along the way, she'd stopped just being Jeff's sister to safeguard and became the woman Mark would do anything to shield.

He couldn't make sense of how he and Cassie had so swiftly understood each other, the shorthand observations, the blunt truths and raw secrets. And it had happened so fast, he couldn't trust it. He needed to get out of here and clear his head before reporting for duty. He wasn't ready to answer more of her probing questions or make any promises for a future as uncertain as his.

Cassie murmured something in her sleep and turned, reaching for him blindly. He slid away and stood beside the bed. At the sight of her sweet ass curving out from beneath one of his T-shirts, pain and need and craving pounded through him. It settled so deep in his bones he was afraid the ache would never leave. The pressure of it licked through his blood.

After a moment, her breathing deepened again and her hand fell to the mattress.

Good.

He forced himself to turn away and strode quietly across the room. He pulled on shorts and a T-shirt and grabbed the flight bag containing the extra uniform, gear and the toiletries he always kept ready in his room.

A blaze of sunshine exploded into the space when he eased the door open and slipped outside. It was a warm tropical noon. The asphalt roadway that curved around the bungalows already radiated heat. Below him the sounds of the calming ocean spelled out the end of his mission and his time with Cassie.

Remorse rose, sour in his gullet. He wasn't ready to let her go, but he wasn't in a place to ask her to be with him, either.

Jogging down the veranda steps, he stopped abruptly when a club car hurtled by carrying Captain Vogt, a service member at the wheel. Music blaring, the char-grilled smells of barbecues in the distance and the jabbering voices of the resort's cleanup crew heralded a return to normalcy.

As for him, his life would never be the same. After yesterday's near disaster and his unforgettable night with Cassie, he had to face up to harsh truths.

Was he flight ready after all?

He marched up the hibiscus-lined walkway, and exchanged a brisk nod with a couple of fatigued-looking rescue swimmers. After a hot shower, he headed to the field hospital. Large air-filled, domed tents rose in the open space. The Red Cross symbol broke up the white and marked the main entrance. Mark bypassed a small crowd of islanders in the intake line.

"Lieutenant Commander Sampson here to see Petty Officer Holt."

Nurse Little approached him and her smile was faintly guarded, like something she had forced herself to wear. She was thin, the kind of thin that came from hard work and long hours; her brown hair was cut in a short, practical style and streaked with gray, and she wore a crisp white uniform that looked fresh, though she'd probably already been working for hours.

But her face, as firmly set as it was, betrayed her; she looked exhausted.

"Right this way, Commander. We moved him since last night and are just finishing up his discharge paperwork. His concussion shows no signs of permanent injury and his arm is stabilized."

Despite the reassuring words, the tension banding around Mark's chest refused to lessen.

The smells of strong coffee, disinfectant and freshly laundered bedding permeated the space as he strode past beeping machines and rows of full beds. A woman with a bandaged head cradled a young girl who flopped across her lap while her husband paced on the other side.

Nurses slid past one another bearing medicine, IV bags, dressings and anything else their bulging pockets couldn't fit. Their eyes bright and determined, they exchanged weary smiles with one another.

"Tell me you brought my flight suit," boomed Dylan when Nurse Little halted and Mark stepped around her to his friend's bedside. Dylan sat mostly upright in bed, his ill-fitting hospital gown gaping wide across his massive chest. "I can't leave with my ass hanging out of this dress I'm wearing."

"Thank you," Mark called to Nurse Little's retreating back. He turned and held up his bag. "Got it right here. They say the knock to your head isn't serious since you were already an idiot to begin with. We're wheels up in an hour."

Dylan's lips twisted and his green eyes—cat's eyes, Mark had heard swooning women describe them as— glinted. "Dumbass." He reached a long arm for the bag.

At six foot seven, it wasn't much of a stretch. "What else did you bring? Chocolates? Roses?"

Mark tossed him the iPhone he'd remembered to grab last night off the copter. "Play some 'Candy Crush.' That'll keep you busy for days."

Dylan lifted his cast. "Good thing I'm a righty or this would really suck."

"It already sucks." Mark raked a hand through his hair, guilt bearing hard on him. "Should never have happened."

"Eh. I get a vacation." After a swig of water, Dylan's eyes swerved to Mark. "Cassie held her own yesterday."

Mark shrugged. "She's not flying again."

"She did a hell of a job."

"She's not flying again," he growled and Dylan threw one large hand up. Mark had gone through that hell yesterday and would never, ever do it again. The only upside to the mission ending and Cassie leaving in a couple of days was knowing she'd fly back to safe, secure Idaho.

"Whoa. Slow down, cowboy. Was just an observation." Dylan accepted a paper cup of pills from a nurse and gulped down his medication. "So I'm flying home today. How about you guys?"

"A couple more days unless I hear otherwise." He scooted out of the departing caregiver's way.

Dylan nodded. "Then I'll see you back in the States."

"Take care, bud."

"Hey. Sign my cast." Dylan's eyebrow arched as he jabbed him in the chest with the plaster. "Something dirty that will make the nurses blush."

He scrawled "something dirty," chucked the Sharpie

at Dylan and flipped a hand in goodbye, chuckling at his friend's protests as he strode away.

Time to make the call he'd been battling since Jeff's death. He'd fought hard to return to the air, but after yesterday's episode, he knew he wasn't ready. Flying without confidence was selfish and dangerous. "So others may live" meant that your first sacrifice might be yourself.

He and his command boss would have a tough conversation.

"Sir. Sir!"

Mark jerked to a stop in the hospital aisle and spied a stooped older man whose broad smile revealed spotted gums. "Can I help you?"

"Yes. Yes. My grandson, Vincent Jameson. He is here."

A lanky young man lay on the hospital cot, his eyes half-shut. He raised his hand and then dropped it, as if a puppeteer had cut his strings.

When Mark noticed the missing lower half of his right leg he winced, remembering the crew member they'd rescued yesterday. Jameson. He'd filled it out on his report himself. His eyes flew back to Vincent. Had to be him.

"I'm sorry," Mark began. Vincent lifted his hand and made an okay sign before his eyes drifted shut. A deep line appeared between the old man's eyebrows, which were startlingly white against his dark skin.

"Why would you be sorry, son? We are celebrating. Stay. Wait. His mother, Marguerite. Here she comes."

A plump woman with closely cropped brown hair hurried up the aisle carrying something in her hand. She looked to be Mark's mother's age. Her floral-print skirt swayed around her sandaled feet and her long neck rose from a bright shirt with a stitched flower emblem. When she spotted Mark, her sudden wide smile filled him with confusion.

After a fast exchange with the older man, she turned to Mark, beaming, and held out a small chamois leather bag.

"I—uh—" He looked down at the stitched-together top. What was it? "Thank you."

Marguerite covered his hand with her own and wrapped his fingers around the soft cloth.

"This is a Mojo hand. You've heard of it?"

He shook his head.

The older man stepped forward. "It will bring you good luck."

"Blessings," Marguerite added. "We want you to have all the good fortune that you've given us."

It was a little late for that, but he was touched. "I appreciate it." He turned the lumpy bag over in his hand, wondering at what was inside. "How's Vincent?"

"He's alive!" The older man's voice rose and a few nearby patients and caregivers stopped to look at them. Marguerite shot him a significant look from beneath lowered brows.

"Yes, but…" Mark's voice trailed off. What should he say? He had no clue.

"Last year this time, I lost my husband." Marguerite twisted a silver ring on her wedding finger, her voice soft. "I have no other children. My father-in-law, Gerald." She nodded at the elderly man. "He has no other children, either, so Vincent is all we have. You gave him back to us."

"You're our savior," Gerald stage-whispered, his attempt to keep down the volume turning just as many heads as his last outburst and earning him another glare from his daughter-in-law.

Mark held back a disbelieving laugh. He wouldn't minimize their feelings. "Cassie, our flight nurse, and Dylan, our rescue swimmer, are the ones to thank. I was just doing my job."

Marguerite's long nails lightly scraped his forearm when she patted him. "And you do it well. Vincent told us how it was. The wind, the boat going down. If you weren't there in time…" Her voice snuffed out like a pinched candle flame. She turned away for a moment.

A weathered hand trembled on Mark's shoulder. "We are so grateful to you. So grateful for returning him to us."

Mark met Gerald's slightly bulging eyes, trying to summon the right words. And then they came, a powerful rushing release, like a flash flood or a burst dam.

"You're welcome."

His eyes stung when Marguerite whirled and hugged him. "Please. Tonight. Come to Iggy's, our bar. Ask William, who works at your resort. He'll take you. We're having a party to celebrate and we're inviting your crew. You're all our guests of honor."

For the first time in days, a heavy weight crushing his chest eased away. He'd considered yesterday's mission a failure because of the injuries to Dylan and Vincent. And, of course, because of Cassie's close call. But perhaps he'd missed the bigger picture, not just with this rescue, but with his career. Losses were a part of his job, even heavy-hitting ones like Jeff's drowning. Maybe one unsuccessful mission or judgment shouldn't define him when he was capable of doing far more good.

He'd trained hard for his job and put everything he had into it every single day. Superior officers had recommended him. Spent time sharing their knowledge so he would do his job well.

Was he really ready to discount their faith in him?

What if he'd already faced the worst the job had to offer and he was walking away before he used that experience to make more saves?

Maybe he needed to stop focusing on the losses. Start remembering the gains. The good he could still do.

"I'd like to come," he said, his thoughts already returning to Cassie. He wanted to celebrate this with her. If they could spend time together without him reliving yesterday's nightmare, maybe he'd be able to think about making some plans for after the mission.

And Cassie would feature in every one of them.

CASSIE WOBBLED ATOP a paddleboard and shoved wet hair out of her eyes. One more plunge and she'd call it quits, no matter how good it felt to be outside on her day off. She was hopeless at this.

A steady breeze dried the droplets sliding down her back and cooled her skin despite the late-afternoon sunshine. The sparkling light transformed Bolongo Bay's surface into a brilliant pavé diamond.

Yellow-striped fish darted in the aquamarine water while orange starfish and conch lined the ridged bottom fifteen or so feet below. Children's shrieks competed with the crying gulls that swooped and glided over the ocean. Scurrying sandpipers raced from a toddler before flapping away into the fading blue of the sky. At the little one's bemused expression, Cassie laughed. It felt great to be free. If only Mark could have joined her.

Why hadn't he woken her before leaving?

Had he been called on an urgent mission and wanted to let her sleep in?

Or did he have second thoughts?

She dipped her oar and propelled herself farther along the ruffled water, parallel to the white beach. The bay was "mushy" just as the beach rental owner promised, meaning long, smooth waves. They nudged her board up and down and her feet rolled along with it. Falling into a rhythm, she sluiced through the sea and let her mind wander.

Last night had been incredible. Yet Mark's guarded answers to her questions made her worry. What if he wasn't ready for a relationship? His leaving without waking her only strengthened her suspicions.

Would he want to see her again after the mission?

When a motorboat hummed by her, she pulled up her paddle and bent her knees as she'd been instructed, anticipating the wake that quickly bumped her board. She rocked unsteadily with the ocean, eyes lingering on the sun as it dipped lower on the horizon.

The way Mark had watched her, gaze sharp and exquisitely intense, the tender way he'd held her… Deep down, he must care.

She'd find him later and talk. Figure things out before they ran out of time.

A parrotfish, its rainbow-colored scales iridescent as it floated nearby, startled her and she nearly lost her paddle. So beautiful. The fragile-looking fish had survived the storm and so had she.

Likewise, the rental shop on the beach was repairing its roof but back in business. Life was going on—a message she needed to take to heart to manage her grief when she got back home.

The sun on her shoulders reminded her of one of Jeff's one-arm hugs. She stared skyward until her eyes watered, hoping her brother smiled down at her. It was still hard to accept his death when she felt like he could call her at any minute, or text her a goofy photo of himself from a mission on the other side of the continent.

But, at last, she'd made peace with his loss.

If he were here, he'd be off and racing with his board, not cautiously edging through the rippling water like she did, spending more time soaked then dry. A couple of kids broke the surface a yard ahead of her board's tip, their dark hair stuck to their skulls. In an instant, they dove again and were gone, their thrashing making her board buck and her feet skid.

The water closed over her head and her ankle strap jerked her back to the surface. She tossed her arms across the green-and-yellow-patterned board and treaded water.

She should have taken the complimentary lesson offered when she'd rented the board, but she'd been in a hurry to make the most of her time off. To live and explore as Jeff had begged her to.

Funny how she'd thought the field hospital pace exhilarating compared to her father's medical practice. Now, after flying a SAR mission, she knew she wanted even more. Not just from Mark, she realized, but for herself, too.

How could she have it all? Her mother had nearly had a coronary when Cassie had announced her plans to come on the mission. Did she dare pursue a real career in the Coast Guard? A smile ghosted across her face as she imagined Jeff's thumbs-up. Tomorrow, she would seek out Nurse Little and ask about options for her future. She wanted to work with a SAR unit.

What was more, it wasn't because of Jeff's prompting. She wanted it for herself now. This mission had been about walking in his path and following his advice, but now she'd make her own way—forge her own direction.

Would Mark support her? He'd praised her work on the *Sea Monarch*…

Out of nowhere, something grabbed her legs and she shrieked. Mark broke the surface, his hair plastered to his head, already laughing. Her yell turned from frightened to outraged.

"You!" she sputtered.

He couldn't stop laughing as he treaded the water beside her. His boyish expression made him look open and happy and incredibly handsome. The dipping sun reflected in his eyes. Drops of water sparkled on his eyelashes. His white teeth flashed in a broad, piratical grin. Eventually, she gave in and laughed with him.

And then she noticed his bare chest. Want suctioned her mouth dry as her eyes wandered over his strong shoulders and pecs before drifting down to his lean torso and waist. He stole her breath. She longed to let him hold her up instead of the board.

Carpe diem.

He caught her waist and she ripped her ankle strap's Velcro loose to wrap her legs around him, her ankles crossing at his spine. Suddenly, the world fell away. Bird cries and the sound of the gentle waves grew muffled. Distant.

"Hello, you," he murmured as he swam them closer to shore until he could stand. Then lazily, yet deliberately, he tilted his head forward and stared into her eyes, his fingers stroking the sensitive skin beneath her chin where the water lapped. He must have been taller than she thought to stand above this water...

Her entire body hummed and a fuzzy sensation filled her head, making it hard to focus. Mark slipped his hand from her chin to cradle her head. His fingers tunneled through her hair, making the back of her neck tingle with anticipation as the pad of his thumb whispered against her cheek. His lips hovered right next to hers and his warm breath heated her face.

Blood pounded so wildly in her veins, she wondered if he could sense the vibration. The hum of sexual energy he always aroused in her returned and lodged squarely between her thighs.

He slowly bent down and his mouth brushed hers, gentle, so achingly tender that it made her squirm and arch against him. She kissed him back, running her hands through his wet hair, her head singing with the thought that he'd sought her out after all.

"Hello," she said a moment later when he'd pulled back. His hands smoothed up and down her sides and she shuddered with pleasure at his touch. "Busy day?"

"Mmm-hmm," he murmured against her temple, and then, as if he couldn't help himself, he skimmed light, shivery kisses along her cheek and jaw.

"Mark." Her voice dipped in warning. Despite the

relative emptiness of the beach, someone they knew could pass by.

His crooked smile made her heart tumble. "Right. Decorum at all times." He feigned such an unconvincing innocent look that it made her giggle.

"I looked for you when I woke up."

Mark's expression sobered and he slid a hand up her slick back. "I should have woken you."

"You wanted to let me rest."

He shook his head. When a salted gust tossed his hair in his face, he shoved it back. "I needed time to think." His eyes delved into hers, then he added, "About us."

Words guaranteed to place a clammy hand around her heart. "And?" A small motorboat whined to life and the two-man vessel appeared beyond the cliffs to their right. She watched the departing fisherman, gathered her nerves and forged on. "What do you think?"

His eyes brightened, the effect more vivid than the now sinking sun that colored the sky pink and gold. "Will you go out with me tonight?"

Her blood rioted at his question and the slippery sleek feel of his muscular body against hers. "What time? I return this in a half hour."

He cupped her face. "I'll pick you up at your room."

She nodded, losing herself in his sincere gaze. Leaning close, she whispered, "Don't be late," against his mouth, tasting the salt on it. His final kiss left her lips tingling and her body warm long after he dove into the water and disappeared.

AN HOUR AND a half later, her reflection gazed back at her. She hardly recognized the sparkle-eyed, flushed woman. Her blond hair had dried into long, humidity-fueled waves that tumbled over her mostly bare shoulders. The pink floral material of the sundress she'd purchased in the resort's gift shop dipped low over her breasts. She considered shortening the spaghetti straps and then let it go. She wanted to look sexy for Mark.

At a quick rap on the door, she shoved her feet into her wedge sandals, grabbed her bag and a cardigan, and hurried to open it.

Mark's instant smile set off a chain reaction of excitement followed by something more dangerous. A craving that went deeper than physical satisfaction. A longing to have him for more than a night.

Her feelings were running deep. She needed to be careful, but it was hard to hold back.

The spicy musk of his cologne and the clean soapy scent of his skin made her toes curl. He smelled so good. It was tempting to drag him inside and forget about this date…

"Ready?" he asked, peering at the bed behind her, his eyes so full of longing, she guessed he was thinking the same thing.

She shouldered her purse. *Talk first. Hot monkey sex later*, she promised herself with a cheeky grin. "Ready," she said, locking the door to her room, and then followed him down the veranda steps. "Where are we going?"

Mark held open the rear door of a small van and followed her inside. "Iggy's. They're having a party."

"All set?" called the driver, a man Cassie had seen around the resort property.

"Set, William. Thanks," Mark responded.

Fifteen minutes later, they bumped to a stop at a

gray weathered structure. A sign with a faded cartoon iguana swung from chains and colored lights twinkled along a sloping eave in the growing dusk. An infectious beat poured from its open door, out onto the porch where islanders leaned on the railing or rocked in brightly painted chairs. Rob and Larry waved but otherwise didn't stop chatting up a couple of gals.

"I'm invited, too," William said after he cut the engine. "When you're ready to leave just let me know."

"Thanks." Taking her hand, Mark led her up the stairs and into a low-ceilinged room with exposed beams and rough floors. A bar ran along one wall and a headphone-wearing DJ nodded along to an upbeat tune that grabbed Cassie's hips and made them sway. A small crowd hung out by the bar, but most of the jumbled conversations seemed to be coming through the two open doorways that flanked it.

"Let's go outside." They stepped into the balmy evening where a dirt-trampled dance floor, filled with grooving islanders, dominated the cleared space. Small tables lined the square and a woman stood and waved excitedly when she caught sight of Mark.

And in that instant, they became a part of the Jameson clan. Cassie lost count of the number of hugs and handshakes she exchanged with grateful relatives who praised her and Mark for all that they'd done to save Vincent.

Hearing her name connected to the words *courageous*, *brave* and *lifesaver* filled her with sharp, sweet pleasure. There, amongst the thankful crowd, Jeff's words came back to her. *Live a little*, he'd said. Somehow she'd always thought he meant to have fun, get out more. Now she interpreted his words differently:

make a difference. Or maybe that was just her trans-
lation. Either way, she couldn't go back to her old life.
It'd shrunk two sizes too small for her.

When the old Culture Club tune "I'll Tumble 4 Ya"
blared, the crowd shrieked and, to Cassie's amazement,
they formed a conga line, Dylan and Larry at the lead,
which left her and Mark alone at last.

They stared at each other. And suddenly, unexpect-
edly, they both started to laugh. "Come on, Cassie!"
He caught her hand and pulled her after him, jogging
to join the swaying line as it sashayed past them.

They cha-cha-cha-ed around the bay-tree-lined
clearing where yellow cuckoos perched, scanning the
ground for dropped tidbits. The birds squawked and
flapped overhead, occasionally making Cassie duck as
she held on to Mark's hand and danced.

With the sky now awash with stars, someone had lit
candles on the tables and torches at each corner of the
property, casting an ambient glow. The song switched
up and the pulsing rhythm separated the line into a gy-
rating mass, Mark and Cassie at its center.

They danced until she stopped feeling self-conscious
and sweat came through their clothes and their hair
stuck to their heads, and her sides hurt so much she
wondered if she'd even be able to work a full shift tomorrow. They danced as if they had nothing else to
do but dance.

And after so many serious, tension-filled days, it
felt good.

She'd forgotten the joy of just existing, of losing herself in music, in a crowd of people, the sensations that
came with becoming one communal, organic mass,
alive only to the pulsing beat. For a few electric, thump-

ing minutes, she let go of everything, her problems floating away like helium balloons—her undecided future, her anxious parents, her frightening feelings for Mark…

She became alive, moving, blissful. She looked at Mark, his eyes sparkling with that peculiar mixture of concentration and freedom that came when someone lost themselves in rhythm.

At last, Mark pulled her away and she held her aching sides, not sure if the pain was from the exercise or the nonstop laughing.

"Having trouble keeping up?" she gasped up at him.

His lips lifted in a wicked smile. "We both know stamina's not a problem for me."

She trailed her fingers up his lean abdomen. "No complaints there."

"Follow me." He captured her hand and led her through the trees down to a rocky outcropping about six feet above the gently rolling sea.

The dusky sky had finally abdicated to an inky black, and the dim shapes of scurrying crabs, darting in and out of stones, caught her eye. Mark sat on a boulder and settled her between his legs. She leaned against his hard chest.

The wind had picked up a little, and it whistled low and steady over the rocks. Down on the sand, a shaggy dog raced back and forth in overexcited circles, leaping and twisting into the air to catch pieces of driftwood thrown by its owner as they passed by.

Cassie closed her eyes and burrowed in, trying to clear her head, trying to focus on the elation of being close to Mark again. Trying not to listen to her thoughts, to acknowledge the complications.

But she couldn't ignore them. Not with her and Mark parting ways in a couple of days. Would she never see him again? The weight of that possibility settled like an icy stone in the pit of her stomach. She shivered.

"You're cold," Mark said in her ear and tightened his arm around her. The water before them winked in the growing starlight.

"No. Thinking," she said, trying to form the words her fear scrambled. She slipped on her cardigan.

"Me, too. I want to get together again, Cassie. When we're stateside."

At the searing intensity in his voice, she turned in his arms. Her eyes met his, and in that split second—as a cloud moved off the moon and illuminated the space with light—she tried to convey to him everything she felt, everything she wanted from him. What she'd learned about them and herself.

"When I came on this mission, I never imagined discovering so much," she began haltingly, wanting to get this right. "I used to play it safe, didn't challenge myself, believed I was happy. No, content."

"And now?" He gazed at her, his eyes soft, the emotion in them making her tremble as his hands traced the bare skin of her legs.

"I want to see you again, too. But I also want this." She nodded at the ocean where two fishermen unloaded their boats, hauling their catch over the side with well-practiced ease. How would Mark take this news? Yesterday's mission had been touch and go, but she'd been successful. He must see the change in her. Know that she was capable.

Mark's dark eyebrows drew together. "I don't understand."

"I don't want to go back to Idaho. I'm going to talk to Nurse Little about getting a medevac job. See if she'll recommend me when I apply to work with a SAR unit. To continue Jeff's legacy." Cassie stopped and shook her head. No. That wasn't exactly right. "To start my own legacy." What her brother had wanted for her all along.

Mark's sharp frown caught her off guard. "What about what happened yesterday?"

"I helped save Vincent and the other sailors." She scooted away from his rigid body, a heavy chill settling in her chest.

He sunk his eyes into hers, his anguish shaking her resolve. "And nearly died."

"I'd rather take those risks than not really live at all."

"I'll make you happy. You don't need that."

She stared up into his fierce, earnest face and gradually, with the inevitable force of a slow-motion punch, it hit her. It wouldn't be enough. "I do. I need both."

His hands dropped from her arms and his jaw tightened. "What if you can't have both? Which would you choose?"

Silence and tension crackled between them, making everything inside her contract. She wrapped her cardigan tighter around her against the cooling night and listened to the swell and hiss of the tide dragging the pebbles in its loose-fingered embrace.

"Don't make me choose." Her stomach churned and she pressed a hand to it.

Mark pinched the bridge of his nose and spoke with his eyes shut. "Yesterday wrecked me. It was bad enough going through that once. I can't fly, do my job, while I'm wondering how you're doing, imagining the worst. Worrying about losing you."

"You said I did a good job. Why won't you support me? Why can't you understand why this is important?" she cried, biting back tears. Her joints ached as the pain of being misunderstood settled in them. He didn't know her as well as she'd thought he did. Why couldn't he see how much this mattered?

"I almost quit today." His quiet words fell through the evening hush and he lowered his head. "But realizing I'd gotten through yesterday gave me more faith in myself," he continued and she released a breath she hadn't known she held.

"I'm glad."

He nodded without lifting his head. The knots of muscle in the corners of his jaw jumped. His voice, when it came, was gruff, broken. "But how can I keep testing that resolve every day knowing that you're also putting yourself at risk?"

"I'll have to deal with that, too. Knowing I could lose you." Her body tightened like a wrung towel and she clenched up, dread rising in her throat.

His eyes opened and the deep sadness in their depths rubbed her heart raw. "I've trained half my life for my career—I want to keep it. But your decision, it feels rushed. Please reconsider."

Cassie's protest lodged in her throat and she gripped her shaking hands together. Never had she wanted anything as much as she wanted Mark, but having him would only be living half a life and she'd vowed never to do that again.

"I care about you, but I can't shortchange my own dreams for someone else again. I won't." The last word cut through the steamy air between them like a cold blade. She heard her own voice fade to a whisper as she waited for his answer.

They were quiet for a dozen painful heartbeats.

When he didn't respond, she took a deep, shaky breath and pulled herself together with all the strength that she had. She forced herself to pick up her bag and scoot off the rock, her skin prickling, waiting for him to reach for her... A piece of her died when he didn't even try to stop her.

When she ducked through the trees, she caught sight of William and flagged him down.

"Can I get a ride?"

"Sure. What about Mark?"

"He'll find his own way," she muttered when she caught sight of Larry, then followed William to the front of the pub.

Mark would find his own path and so would she. Apart. The thought tore open her chest, splintered her heart, its fragments shredding her.

She dropped her head to her knees and screwed her eyes shut when Iggy's disappeared from view. A vise wrapped around her lungs and squeezed. She felt like she was suffocating and gasped for air. Her breath filled her ears and she cried silently in the backseat until her chest heaved and her stomach muscles hurt, oblivious to all except losing the man who'd built her up, only to tear her apart, again.

12

CASSIE RUBBED GRITTY eyes the next morning then grabbed the field hospital's large can of coffee, groggy and miserable. Her hand shook as she measured out the grounds into the filter. How many tablespoons for strong coffee? Two per cup. So forty-eight ounces of water meant...

Crap.

The brown particles overflowed the measuring cap and filled the filter. Too much? A tear plopped onto the counter in front of her. She wiped her cheek with her palm and put the measurer down. It took her some minutes to see clearly again. Whatever she'd poured, it'd have to do.

She carried the carafe to the sink, twisted on the faucet and held it beneath the gushing water. Her chest felt like a crash site, flares of pain surrounding the crater where her heart had been. Everything she'd let herself hope for, Mark had crushed beneath one regulation-issue boot last night. How could everything have fallen apart so quickly, a house of cards when she'd dreamed of building a life together?

Water sloshed on the counter when she poured it into the reservoir and placed the carafe on the warming plate. She flicked the switch and stared at the machine. It started to gurgle, spit, then flow, the sharp aroma filling the nurses station.

She pressed her fingertips to her throbbing forehead and leaned against the counter. Was Mark as miserable as she was? Did he regret the decision that'd ripped them apart? Every time she thought of it, the tear inside her chest widened. At any moment, she expected to fall apart, cleaved in half.

"Cassie?" Nurse Little appeared in the rear entrance. "You're not on for an hour. What brings you here?"

"I hoped we could chat before my shift?" Her voice rose at the end, a question. She needed to focus on her future...not her crushing loss.

The older woman nodded, pulled a red mug off a metal rack, poured out the ink-black coffee and joined Cassie, her rubber soles squeaking on the floor. She waved away the steam rising off the surface of her mug before closing her eyes and taking a long drink.

"Strong," she sputtered then opened her eyes, her gray gaze sharp and assessing. "What can I do for you?"

Cassie's hands twisted beneath the table and she willed back the relentless tears that gathered in her eyes. "I'm interested in becoming an emergency medical technician and survival flight nurse."

Her supervisor ripped open a sweetener packet and tapped the white powder into her coffee. The spoon clanked against the china's sides as she stirred.

"I think that's a wise decision."

Cassie blinked at her. "You do?"

"I've watched you, Cassie." She placed her wet spoon precisely on a napkin and gripped her mug handle. "At first, I wasn't sure about you, despite your advanced credentials. A lot of volunteers lose their enthusiasm once the hard work begins. Yet you asked for even more responsibility with the SAR flight. I'm told you conducted yourself quite well." She sipped her coffee.

An image of Mark flashed in Cassie's mind and the space he'd vacated rose empty and dark inside her. She shoved down the sensation. Time to focus on herself. Her life. Her rules. "Who shared that information?"

"Lieutenant Commander Sampson when he stopped by yesterday. Shoot." A drop of coffee spilled on the counter and she dabbed at it.

"And—" Cassie cleared her throat, astonished. She began again. "What did he say?"

Nurse Little tossed out the damp napkin. "He said you conducted yourself professionally. I also learned that you boarded the ship?"

Cassie's chin rose and her heart swelled. So Mark had complimented her. Thought well of her skills… If only that translated into real action. Faith in her.

"I did. One of the rescue swimmers became injured and I was needed to triage as well as treat a critical patient."

"Vincent Jameson." They both looked up when the field hospital's air filter hummed to life overhead. "You saved his life."

Cassie nodded slowly. Saving Vincent had felt like rescuing her brother in a way. The sense of accomplishment had finally replaced the impotent, helpless feeling that'd gripped her since Jeff's disappearance.

"I'd like to do more, but I'm not sure about my next steps. My plan is to join the Coast Guard. I know it's not the Red Cross, but I hoped you might have some advice to share with me."

Reaching into her uniform pocket, her superior produced a postcard with a picture of a cat holding an SOS sign. "Before I left for Saint Thomas, a nurse I mentored sent me this. She's with the Coast Guard and mentioned that the paramedic training program she teaches is open again. It only happens about once every couple of years, and they're always interested in recruiting from the Red Cross."

Her eyes glinted. She rose and crossed to the sink, her now empty mug in hand. "The program starts next week, though. You'd need to be able to fly straight to Petaluma, California, from here."

"How would I be approved that quickly?" Cassie gasped, thinking how fast things were lining up now that she'd finally figured them out...all except Mark.

"I can pull a few strings when I need to." Nurse Little's mouth curved slightly and her eyebrows rose a fraction of an inch. "You already have your Certified Flight Registered Nurse designation, so that makes you attractive, as well as your Certified Emergency Nurse and Basic Trauma Life Support training. I believe you'll need ninety flight hours, training in Prehospital Advanced Life Support, and Advanced Trauma Life Support certification. I wouldn't be surprised if you're assigned straight out of the program."

Suddenly light-headed, Cassie gripped the back of her chair and blew out a shaky breath.

The senior nurse ran the tap and glanced over her shoulder. "Too much?"

"No. No. It's what I want."

"Good. I'd be glad to give you a recommendation, as would Lieutenant Commander Sampson, I'm certain."

Cassie frowned. A conundrum if there ever was one. "I'm not so sure he'd be willing to do that."

After returning the washed mug to the rack, Nurse Little dried her hands and turned. "It'd be no problem at all, and I'm happy to speak to him or another member of the crew…his copilot, perhaps, if that's preferable."

Her heart began to thump. "I would appreciate that. It's been an honor to work with you and the Red Cross. It—ah—actually inspired me to do this."

To Cassie's surprise, Nurse Little pulled Cassie to her feet and enfolded her in a quick, Dial-soap-infused hug. "We were lucky to have you. I'll be watching what's sure to be a distinguished career."

Cassie smiled back. "Thanks. I'll keep in touch." Speaking of which… "Would I be able to call home?" She pictured her mother. Heard the conversation in her mind and realized that as far as she'd come, she still had one last battle to fight to complete her transformation.

Nurse Little handed her a large cordless phone. "Dial 811 for command center and they'll connect you to the right number. You can use my office for privacy." She gestured to the small cubby to the left of the nurses station. Cassie looked up when her supervisor squeezed her shoulder. "Good luck."

"Thank you."

Slightly out of breath, Cassie scooted into the space, closed the curtains for privacy and stared at the phone.

If she went through with this, she was as good as throwing in the towel with Mark. Grief overwhelmed her. It tore at her heart and her stomach and her head and it pulled her under, and she honestly didn't think she could bear it. A life minus the man she loved... Would she come to resent her dream career without him?

Was this all an impulsive mistake?

Cassie's thoughts spun as they always had in the past, refusing to settle. For a moment, her familiar indecisiveness returned and she worried she'd end up doing nothing at all. Then like a roulette ball falling into a slot, everything clicked.

No. She wouldn't have walked away from Mark, or broached the subject with her supervisor, unless deep down she knew this was the right choice, tough as it was.

Her mother would be shocked.

She might have a breakdown.

Cassie's hand tightened on the receiver. Yes, both of those things might happen. But she couldn't, wouldn't, live her life to make others happy. And deep down, wasn't that really just an excuse not to make decisions at all? As long as she was accountable to everyone else, she never had to be accountable to herself.

No one—not even Mark—could shape her destiny. Her body felt pummeled from the inside out over how sad, hurt and disappointed she felt, but she had to move on. Time to take ownership of her life.

A moment later, a distant ringing sounded in Cassie's ear.

"Hello?" At her mother's familiar voice, tears rushed to Cassie's eyes, along with a longing for home. And she wouldn't see it for some time if Nurse Little's confidence proved reliable.

"Mom." Cassie opened her mouth to continue, but her mother interrupted her.

"Cassie! I've been waiting by the phone all week. Are you coming home soon? I baked and froze chocolate chip, peanut butter and shortbread cookies."

"Don't forget the snickerdoodles," Cassie's father broke in after a click sounded, heralding another line being picked up.

"Wow. You've been busy," Cassie said, faintly. She dumped all of the paper clips out of their dispenser and began sorting them into two piles by size.

"I had to keep my mind off…well… I'll feel better when you're home."

"There's something I need to tell you." Cassie dropped a large paper clip on her growing pile and closed her eyes. Took a deep breath. "I'm not coming home because I've decided to join the Coast Guard as a nurse. A training program begins on Monday in California."

"S-say that again?" her mother murmured. Cassie pressed the phone to her warm ear.

"I want to be a flight nurse." She leaned forward and rested her elbows on the small desk, lowering her voice when the sounds of nurses changing shifts filtered through the curtain. "I filled in for one of the Jayhawk crew's flight medics. It was incredible."

"Incredible?" Her mother's voice rose.

"Joyce," warned Cassie's father. "Hear her out. Does this have to do with Jeff?"

A long silence descended. Because of her mother's fragile mental health, they'd mostly avoided talking about him since the memorial.

"Yes," Cassie admitted. She scooped the large paper

clips and dropped them into the holder. "At first. But now I want this for myself."

"You don't have to prove anything," insisted her father.

"Yes, I do." The last of the small paper clips slipped through her fingertips into a bowl. "All my life I've tried making everyone happy. I thought I was doing something good, the right thing. But I wasn't noble. I was a coward."

"There's nothing wrong with being cautious." Cassie heard the splash of liquid hitting the bottom of a glass. The image of her mother pouring the juice she took with her pills rose.

Scooching farther back in the wooden chair, she sat up straighter. "I want to make a difference. Help people in desperate situations. I can't do that in my old job."

"It used to make you happy."

"No, it didn't" came her father's firm reply and Cassie's mouth dropped open. "She was miserable there, Joyce. We both saw it. Why do you think she took all those extra courses? She wanted more. We just didn't want to admit it."

"You weren't happy living here, honey?" The sadness in her mother's voice made Cassie's eyes sting.

"I was. But I want more. I can do more. I helped to save people from a sinking ship."

"Oh, my good Lord," gasped Cassie's mother. "You could have died yourself."

"Yes." No sugarcoating it. Not anymore. She picked up a pen and began doodling to get rid of her nervous energy. "But I've never felt more alive."

"You're lucky you got out of there," observed her father, his voice deep with concern.

"Jeff's old crew manned the Jayhawk that carried me. The pilot, Mark, he's uh—not such a bad guy."

"He left Jeff."

"He saved Cassie."

Her parents spoke at the same time and then a long silence descended.

"And is it this Mark that convinced you to join the Coast Guard?" Joyce asked after what sounded like a hefty swallow.

If it wasn't so sad, Cassie would have laughed. "Hardly. He doesn't want me anywhere near it."

Her heart squeezed.

"He sounds like a sensible fellow."

"And controlling. He doesn't understand how important this is to me." Her pencil's tip broke on the paper.

Another lengthy quiet descended, and then her mother said, "I've got to go."

"Mom. Mom?" Cassie's stomach ached when she didn't get a response. She hated to hurt her mother. "Dad, I should let you go so you can comfort her."

"I will, but there's something I want to say first."

Cassie braced herself.

"I'm proud of you, honey. We only get one shot at life and you need to do what makes you happy."

Without Mark, would she be happy? "Thanks, Dad. That means a lot."

"You're going to help a lot of people," her father said. "Jeff would be proud, too."

"I love you, Dad." Cassie's voice broke. "Tell Mom I love her, too."

"I will. Once she's had time to process this, she'll come around." Her father's reassuring tone settled Cassie's rising fear before they disconnected.

Cassie stared at the phone she'd set on the desk. Gratitude for her father's understanding swelled. It'd gone better that she'd expected. Still, the victory felt hollow since Mark would never celebrate it with her.

Needing to clear her head, Cassie stepped outside for a few minutes before her shift started. At the distant thrum of a motorboat, she studied the rippling water, the strings of buoys that marked the boating channels and, on the far side, the tree-covered hills stretching up to the blue sky.

The familiar sound of a helicopter erupted overhead and she blinked into the rising sun at a Jayhawk whirring out to sea.

Mark. She couldn't know for sure, but deep down it felt like him leaving her, even though they weren't scheduled to leave until tomorrow.

A child tore down the beach with a dog at her heels. Their delighted howls pinged inside the empty cavity Mark had left inside her. Everything felt wrong with her body.

Overwhelming tiredness weighted her bones, and a heaviness in her lungs made it hard to breathe. An extreme emotion erupted inside her and it was all she could do not to roar.

Instead, her mouth worked silently before one word emerged at last. "Goodbye."

13

One month later

MARK STARED OUT the window of the Elizabeth City
Coast Guard station's commissary, absently chewing a
dry turkey sandwich. Service personnel wearing dress
blues, more casual trops or flight suits surrounded him.
Occasional bursts of laughter punctuated the steady
babble that filled the house-size room. The whine of
an engine sounded through the glass and he tracked
a rolling Herc as it taxied to its distant runway, the
bright sunlight glinting off its white-and-orange sides.
How many missions had he flown since he'd last seen
Cassie?

Fifty-seven and a half hours, twenty days of flying,
three SAR cases, six training flights, ten law enforce-
ment missions, six combo flights, twenty basket/RS
hoists and four night flights. Twelve lives saved, four
assisted.

Still not enough to banish her from his thoughts.
Sometimes he woke up speaking her name. He dropped
his mostly uneaten sandwich and picked up his spoon.

Tomato-scented steam rose from the bowl but it didn't tempt him. Nothing did, unless it was dreams of Cassie, hot and eager beneath him, her body offering him the peace of mind he couldn't find when awake.

He'd volunteered for everything possible since completing the Saint Thomas mission. Had even taken part in some of the training academy's drills, flying for them as he'd once done earlier in his career. Anything to keep his mind occupied, though none of it worked. His final conversation with Cassie ran through his brain on a permanent loop. Her crestfallen face was always before him.

The thing that haunted him, that left his stomach in toxic knots, his food like ashes on his tongue, was the way they'd left things. That they hadn't even said goodbye.

Sending his recommendation to Petaluma should have helped. Given him closure. Stopped him from picturing her in the air, dropping down to ships, in danger. She wasn't his responsibility anymore. Yet somewhere along the line she'd become much more than that.

"Commander." Dylan stopped at Mark's table, his usual smile missing. He wore an olive green flight suit peppered with zippers that held just about anything. It looked like he'd stowed his good humor in one of them. Mark angled his head to meet the tall swimmer's eyes.

"Taking off soon? Kodiak, right?"

Dylan nodded slowly and held out his ACE-wrapped arm. "Homeward bound."

"Maybe they'll have a parade."

One side of Dylan's mouth jerked up. "Run me out of town is more like it."

"Broken laws, broken hearts?"

Dylan shot him a sideways glance. "Something like that."

Interesting. Ian had mentioned a woman there... Still, he knew better than to pry. He stuck out a hand and Dylan shook it firmly. "Good luck. Keep in touch."

"Will do. So Cassie's doing well, huh?"

Mark's heart added an extra beat or three at her name. "What do you mean?"

Dylan's brow furrowed. "You haven't kept in touch?"

He shook his head.

"Idiot." A couple of passing guys clapped Dylan on the back. He nodded at them then frowned down at Mark. "A friend of mine at Cape Cod said she's working with his crew now." When another man waved from the door, Dylan returned the gesture. "Look. I gotta go. But call her, man. Don't be an ass."

"Words to live by."

Dylan snorted. "True enough."

He watched his straight-backed friend disappear and silently wished him well. He'd miss his workout buddy, who also had the good grace to let someone else win at poker once in a while.

"Sampson?"

Mark glanced up to see his old mentor, Frank Gilford, in a bravo jacket, the navy color broken up with ribbons and a name tag with a new designation: Captain. Mark stared. A full bird, O-6. Big-time. It'd been—what—three years since he'd seen the legendary pilot? One of the most decorated aviators in the Coast Guard's history.

In a flash, he stood and saluted. "Congratulations, sir."

Captain Gilford waved away the gesture and sat

heavily in the seat opposite. "Appreciated. Though I think it's their way of saying I'm too old for the cockpit. Time for a desk job."

"Hardly, sir."

The ruddy man squinted at Mark. With his thick brush of gray hair and craggy face, he looked ageless. Not too old to fly. Not by a long shot.

"What brings you here?" Last Mark heard, he'd been stationed in San Diego.

Frank's lips thinned and the skin around them turned white. He drummed thick fingers on the tabletop and looked out the window at the Jayhawks and Dolphins.

"Lost Marie," he said at last. "A year ago. Our kids wanted to get together here with her parents. Hold a memorial…" His voice trailed off and Mark wished he could smack himself upside the head for digging. The poor guy. He'd loved his wife with the kind of devotion Mark had never known himself…before Cassie.

"I'm sorry, Frank."

His gray eyes swerved to Mark. The steely expression Frank usually wore was gone. Instead, he looked… lost, a terrifying feeling for a navigator, Mark knew.

"Brain aneurysm. Just like that." Frank's jaw stiffened and the wrinkles around his eyes deepened. "Doctor said she didn't…she didn't even feel it."

Mark nodded, straining to keep his face neutral. Not overly sympathetic the way he felt. Frank wouldn't want to get weepy in the mess hall. "That's a hell of a thing."

"Always thought it'd be me first." Frank crossed his arms over his broad chest and a muscle jumped in his jaw. "All that time I spent worrying I'd make a widow of her." His voice trailed off and his fingers drummed on his sleeves. At last his hands dropped back into his lap and he looked up. "Guess you never know."

"No guarantees in life."

Frank exhaled in a deep sigh. "The only thing you can—and should—count on is the love of a good woman. I was lucky to have the time I had with her. Wouldn't wish a moment of it away. When you find it, don't waste it, son."

He shoved back his chair and both men stood. Mark watched the door swing shut behind the captain long after they'd shaken hands and Frank had strode away.

Back in his seat, he stared at his food and let his mentor's words sink in. Flying during the hurricane operation had helped him come to terms with what'd happened to Jeff. But being with Cassie, someone who understood his lowest, darkest moment—shared it, too—had pulled him apart and put him together again.

Maybe the time had come for him to quit denying himself what he desired, punishing himself for what he couldn't change, guarding himself against future hurt. With Cassie, he'd felt like the hero he'd tried to become. Saw that he could be that man again.

Most of all, he now saw that he'd been a damn fool. *Don't waste a minute*, Frank had advised.

Mark looked at his watch and thought of Cassie. How much time had passed since he'd last seen her? Too much.

Unknowingly, his old mentor had given Mark the best advice of all. Without Cassie, his days had shrunk somehow. She was a score on his heart. Had been from the moment her iridescent blue eyes met his at Mayday's. She'd dragged him from the dark that night and hadn't let him retreat into it since. She leveled him out. Gave him perspective. Showed him the path to forgiveness, and he was a stronger man for it.

A better man because of her.

Had he been wrong to break things off? Could he have her in his life after all?

After Jeff's death, Cassie had coped with her loss by running toward what'd killed him rather than away. That took courage and guts, which he admired about her, along with her big heart. What a fool to toss it away because of anxiety over things he couldn't control.

Mark grabbed his tray and loaded it onto the moving runner. When he turned, he barreled into a junior officer.

"Hey, what's the…? Oh. Sorry, sir." The younger man jerked and saluted when he caught sight of Mark's name tag.

What's the hurry? Mark completed the thought silently, shoving through the commissary's doors and pacing down the hall, his fast walk becoming a jog that made his pulse jump.

Cassie.

CASSIE HOPPED OFF the Jayhawk and jogged beside the stretcher bearing the severely burned sailor her crew had rescued, along with his three mates, twenty minutes ago.

Medics rushed to meet her on the wet tarmac, radios hissing on their belts. Their neon uniforms reflected the nearby ambulance's spinning blue light.

She reported out quickly in the chilly, unrelenting drizzle, handed over her notes and then backed away as they loaded the critically injured man into the transport. They'd already arranged for him to be airlifted to MedStar's burn center and she sent up a silent wish that his condition wouldn't destabilize on the trip.

Blood pumping in her ears, she watched the shrieking vehicle disappear as water streamed down her face, dripping off her nose. Nearly light-headed with adrenaline, she forced herself to turn away. To let go. One week on her new job and she'd already learned the toughest part…handing her rescues over and stepping back.

Just as she had with Mark…

Her shoes squelched in a puddle and soaked her socks as she headed back to her quarters. Wanting some time to cool down, she waved off the club car that slowed beside her, her crew members offering a lift.

A spray of water kicked up from its wheels and drenched her further.

Nice.

It had rained for a solid two days, turning the skies the color of wet ashes, the grass to mud. When she reached the sidewalk's water-darkened concrete, she stopped to smooth the soaked olive green fabric of her suit, squeezing out some of the water where she twisted it at her waist.

Giving it up as useless, she continued on, not nearly as eager for bed as she should be. With her job still smelling like a new car, she had a hard time coming down from the high it gave her. She loved being a flight nurse. Every day she'd spent this month had only deepened her certainty that she'd chosen the right path.

If only it hadn't taken her away from Mark.

She missed him.

She wished she could see the broad-shouldered man

with the lopsided smile who'd won her heart. But she wouldn't surrender her life, too, as he'd wanted.

Although, she reminded herself, he *had* recommended her for the training program. He'd supported her dreams even if he hadn't wanted to be a part of her life. She wished she could have thanked him for that but there'd been no time. Her world had been moving at high speed ever since she'd applied for the program.

Maybe she should call him. Just to thank him…

How many times had she thought that in the past four weeks? Truly, she needed to put him out of her mind. But it wasn't easy when he permeated her thoughts. Made love to her in her dreams every night until she was breathless and woke up empty, wanting him.

Her drowned-rat reflection followed her in the rows of dark windows that made up the west side of the station's main living quarters. A warm shower and bed. A glass of wine.

That was what she needed.

Then she spied a figure in the distance and jerked to a halt.

"Cassie?" A tall man wearing a formal blue uniform stepped from beneath the overhang, his light golden eyes making her pulse sputter as he swept off his black-brimmed white hat.

"Mark. What are you doing here?" She shoved back her streaming hair and tried to hide the catch in her voice. She couldn't tear her eyes away—the dark hair, the way his shoulders fit in his uniform, those chiseled features that were so achingly familiar to her—its strengths and vulnerabilities, its shape and feel. A raw wound of emotion opened and a muffled sob escaped her. She pressed her arm against her mouth.

He stepped close and she breathed in his spicy, masculine scent. "Are you okay?"

She hesitated, her heart beating erratically as she nodded and met his gaze. His eyes, so long strained and unhappy, looked clear and relaxed. They studied her closely, as if he were storing every molecule of her away.

"Can we talk? Go somewhere?"

She looked down at her sodden clothes and decided on the spot that a shower was the lowest item on her priority list right now.

He extended his umbrella to shield her. "Do you want to change? Dry off?"

The tender, concerned look in his eyes nearly undid her, but she forced herself to shake her head. The rules about having visitors in her dorm were fairly strict, although she still wasn't clear if a fellow serviceman from another base would be considered as such...

Better not take the chance.

Her hand trembled a little when she gestured to a bench beneath a distant open-air pavilion where she'd been told bands sometimes played.

She huddled close under Mark's umbrella, awkward in her soaked uniform, grateful for the sideways rain that cooled her burning cheeks. He'd hurt her heart deeply and she needed to tamp down this rush of emotion. To take care to protect herself, despite how good it felt to be near him again.

Despite the mud rising around her boots and squishing between her laces, her sole focus was on his strong hand pressed to the center of her back as he steered her to the structure.

They ducked underneath the overhang and he led her to a spot on the built-in benches that circled the shadowed space. Overhead, pines whispered conspiratorially, their dense branches shielding the pavilion from the worst of the storm.

Seated, his thigh rested mere inches from hers. Her whole body tingled with awareness.

"We just rescued four off a sailing vessel," she blurted, feeling proud, desperately wanting him to see what she'd accomplished.

"Congratulations." The baritone rumble of his voice made her insides vibrate. Off in the distance, the whirring of an incoming copter sounded. One of the other crews at this busy station.

"I appreciate your letter of recommendation." Despite the damp, her palms began to sweat. His thigh loomed so close. His big hand rested on his knee, and she thought about what it would feel like to place her palm inside his.

"It was the least I could do. You were great on that mission with Dylan. Cool under pressure. You were born to do this."

She blinked at him, beginning to see that maybe he'd come here to do more than apologize. "Say that again."

He shifted closer and moved the hand closest to her, stretching that arm out along the back of the seat without quite touching her. "Cassie, I ran into an old friend who helped me see our relationship differently. I understand now that I was dead wrong to make you choose between me and your career."

"You didn't want to worry about me." She understood that much. Saw now that it was concern, not control, that'd led to their painful breakup.

"And I haven't stopped." Behind her, Mark's hand came to rest on her damp hair where it snaked down her back. She could feel the gentle tug against her scalp as he slid his fingers very lightly up and down its length. "But I realize now that you never know what the future holds. If trying to protect myself from the pain of losing you means not being with you—the most important person in my life—then I've already lost."

Her heart stuck in her throat and her skin hummed with pleasurable shivers.

"What are you saying?" Her breathless voice didn't sound like it belonged to her at all. Hope struck a small light that flickered to life inside her as she stared back at him, waiting for him to continue.

"Not only do I support you as a flight nurse, I'm proud of you, too." He slid his fingers under her hair to cup her shoulder in one hand. "I don't want to lose you." He traced wet patterns on her arm with the tips of her hair. Had he leaned closer? Cassie couldn't quite breathe. Either that or she was holding her breath, waiting for him to kiss her.

"I don't want to lose you, either," she managed, hypnotized by the promise in his light eyes. "No matter how far apart we are."

His hand stilled. "Are you sure?"

"Completely sure."

"Because there's a chance we may not have to worry about that."

Closing the gap between them, she edged over that last inch of seat; her thigh brushed his and her hip bumped him.

"Why is that?" She stroked his cheek with shaky fingers, hardly daring to believe she might have shared her heart with a man who would do anything to care for it.

From the deep pocket of his uniform's overcoat, he produced a plastic bag containing papers. "I'm up for a change in duty stations and I can request to come here, with your consent."

She opened her mouth, but he pressed a finger to her lips. "There's one more thing you need to know before you decide."

"Okay," she mumbled against the finger now tracing her lips.

"I love you," he said simply and his eyes searched hers, his expression heartbreakingly vulnerable.

Mark loved her. He really loved her. Everything else was a detail. Her heart swelled between her ribs, and her lungs burned.

Closing her eyes, she thought of how he had felt, his breath mingling with hers, his arms around her, his body pressed tight against her. She thought of how hard he'd fought, every step of her journey, to keep her safe, how he would always protect her. She realized now that it wasn't a bad thing at all, but a loving thing. And she knew she would do anything to shield him, too.

"I love you, too, Mark."

His eyes blazed at her through the tangle of brown hair that fell across his forehead. He pulled her close, kissing a line from her cheek to her ear and down her neck, inciting shivers.

"Please come." She tipped her head back, enjoying the way the sensations chased down her spine.

When he stopped kissing her, she stared at her one-time enemy turned lifelong love, and felt more complete than she'd ever been.

"Right now?" His brow arched and a wicked gleam entered his eyes.

"Do you know the policy about visitors?" she whispered, heady with the need to feel him inside her.

"I know the policy at my hotel. How long before your next flight?" He grinned lazily, his eyes smoldering.

"Sixteen hours."

His mouth lowered, hovering tantalizingly close. "Should be enough time…just."

He pulled her close and kissed her tenderly. Cassie's eyes drifted closed and she melted against this wonderful man, who'd not only built her back up but helped her transform into something more, someone whole greater than the sum of her parts. She couldn't wait to begin a future where they were both their own hero and each other's.

* * * * *

*Dylan Holt thought he'd left Kodiak, Alaska,
and the girl who broke his heart, behind forever.
But the Coast Guard has other ideas…
and reuniting with Nolee Arnauyq may just be
hot enough to warm the Bering Sea!*

Look for Karen Rock's next sizzling
UNIFORMLY HOT! *story*
HIS LAST DEFENSE in stores April, 2017.

REQUEST YOUR FREE BOOKS!
2 FREE NOVELS PLUS 2 FREE GIFTS!

❦ HARLEQUIN®

Blaze

red-hot reads!

YES! Please send me 2 FREE Harlequin® Blaze® novels and my 2 FREE gifts (gifts are worth about $10). After receiving them, if I don't wish to receive any more books, I can return the shipping statement marked "cancel." If I don't cancel, I will receive 4 brand-new novels every month and be billed just $4.74 per book in the U.S. or $5.21 per book in Canada. That's a savings of at least 14% off the cover price. It's quite a bargain. Shipping and handling is just 50¢ per book in the U.S. and 75¢ per book in Canada.* I understand that accepting the 2 free books and gifts places me under no obligation to buy anything. I can always return a shipment and cancel at any time. Even if I never buy another book, the two free books and gifts are mine to keep forever.

150/350 HDN GH2D

Name	(PLEASE PRINT)	
Address		Apt. #
City	State/Prov.	Zip/Postal Code

Signature (if under 18, a parent or guardian must sign)

Mail to the **Reader Service:**
IN U.S.A.: P.O. Box 1867, Buffalo, NY 14240-1867
IN CANADA: P.O. Box 609, Fort Erie, Ontario L2A 5X3

Want to try two free books from another line?
Call 1-800-873-8635 or visit www.ReaderService.com.

* Terms and prices subject to change without notice. Prices do not include applicable taxes. Sales tax applicable in N.Y. Canadian residents will be charged applicable taxes. Offer not valid in Quebec. This offer is limited to one order per household. Not valid for current subscribers to Harlequin Blaze books. All orders subject to credit approval. Credit or debit balances in a customer's account(s) may be offset by any other outstanding balance owed by or to the customer. Please allow 4 to 6 weeks for delivery. Offer available while quantities last.

Your Privacy—The Reader Service is committed to protecting your privacy. Our Privacy Policy is available online at www.ReaderService.com or upon request from the Reader Service.

We make a portion of our mailing list available to reputable third parties that offer products we believe may interest you. If you prefer that we not exchange your name with third parties, or if you wish to clarify or modify your communication preferences, please visit us at www.ReaderService.com/consumerchoice or write to us at Reader Service Preference Service, P.O. Box 9062, Buffalo, NY 14240-9062. Include your complete name and address.

HB15

*Erick Fields is shocked when prim and proper
Clover Greene agrees that sex should be part of their
"fake boyfriend" deal. She needed a buffer against her
judgmental family, but this Thanksgiving she's getting a
whole lot more!*

Read on for a sneak preview of
HER NAUGHTY HOLIDAY,
book three of Tiffany Reisz's sexy holiday trilogy
MEN AT WORK.

"I'm not going to try to convince you to do something
you don't want to do," Clover said.

"Why not?"

"Because no means no."

"I didn't say no. Come on. I'm a businessman. Let's
haggle."

Clover laughed a nervous laugh, almost a giggle. She
sat behind her desk and Erick sat on the desk next to her.

"You're pretty when you laugh," he said. "But you're
also pretty when you don't laugh."

"You're sweet," she said. "I feel like I shouldn't have
brought this up."

"So do you really need someone to play boyfriend for
the week? It's that bad with your family?"

She sighed heavily and sat back.

"It's hard," she said. "They love me but that doesn't
make the stuff they say easier to hear. They think they're

saying 'We love you and we want you to be happy,' but what I hear is 'You're inadequate, you're a disappointment and you haven't done what you're supposed to do to make *us* happy.'"

He grinned at her and shrugged. "You think I'm cute?" he asked.

"You're hot," she said. "Like UPS-driver hot."

"That's hot."

"Smoking."

"This is fun," he said. "Why haven't we ever flirted with each other before?"

"You know, my parents would probably be very impressed if they thought I were dating a single father. They'd think that was a ready-made family."

"You really want me to be your boyfriend?" Erick asked. He already planned on doing it. He'd do anything for this woman, including but not limited to pretending to be her boyfriend for a couple days.

"I would appreciate it," she said.

"We can have sex all week, too, right?"

"Okay."

"What?" Erick burst into laughter.

"What?" she repeated. "Why are you laughing?"

"I didn't think you'd say yes. I was joking."

"You were?" Her blue eyes went wide.

"Well…yeah. I mean, not that I don't want to. I do want to. I swear to God, I thought you'd say no. I never guessed you'd say yes, not in a million years."

"And why not?"

Don't miss HER NAUGHTY HOLIDAY by Tiffany Reisz, available November 2016 wherever Harlequin® Blaze® books and ebooks are sold.

Reading Has Its Rewards

Earn **FREE BOOKS!**

Register at **Harlequin My Rewards** and submit your Harlequin purchases from wherever you shop to earn points for free books and other exclusive rewards.

Plus submit your purchases from now till May 30th for a chance to win a $500 Visa Card*.

Visit **HarlequinMyRewards.com** today

MYR16R1

HARLEQUIN®

A *Romance* FOR EVERY MOOD™

Love the Harlequin book you just read?

Your opinion matters.

Review this book on your favorite
book site, review site, blog or your own
social media properties and share
your opinion with other readers!

JUST CAN'T GET ENOUGH?

Join our social communities
and talk to us online.

You will have access to the latest
news on upcoming titles and special
promotions, but most importantly,
you can talk to other fans about your
favorite Harlequin reads.

Harlequin.com/Community

Facebook.com/HarlequinBooks

Twitter.com/HarlequinBooks

Pinterest.com/HarlequinBooks